Addie & Gray

CLUB DECADENT BOOK TWO

K.C. FORD

eBook ISBN: 978-1-7780290-7-3

Paperback ISBN: 978-1-0691328-2-6

Cover Design: Katherine Ferguson

Edits: Katherine Ferguson

Formatted with Atticus

About

This is Book Two in the Club Decadent Series. Each book focuses on a specific pairing, and can be read as a standalone. Though **the series is best enjoyed in order.**

Divorced and free from her cheating ex, Addison Carter is more than ready to start over at forty, choosing to embrace her author dreams. When her editor suggests doing some hands-on research, Addie reaches out to her BFF Andrew for a guest pass to the illustrious Club Decadent, New York's most tantalizing adult playground.

Grayson Matthews wasn't exactly looking for love when a violet-haired, blue-eyed, curvaceous beauty walked smack-dab into him in the middle of his club, but he's more than ready to 'seize the day.' With a little help from his matchmaking friend, Gray will do everything to win Addie's heart.

Authors Note

This story is a high-heat, M/F, older woman/younger man, second chance at love, romance with a pleasure Dom who's all about her, and a quirky author who never thought the men in romances could ever be real – spoiler alert – they are! ;) If that's all you needed to know, skip ahead to Chapter One. If you need a little more detail, please refer to the content list on the following page:

Third Person with Dual POV. She's 39-40, He's 34-35. Instalust/Instalove. Tattooed MMC and FMC. Close Proximity. Discussion of scars from physical harm, body insecurity, and body positivity (MMC has combat scars). Discussion of kids – MMC has a vasectomy, FMC has a grown daughter. Secondary character nonbinary rep. They talk about sexual desires, wants, needs, and boundaries (consent is continuously confirmed). Explicit sexual scenes with elements of kink, BDSM, exhibitionism, and voyeurism. Lots of profanity, including tons of 'dirty talk'. Pop culture references. So many 'good girl' vibes. 'There's no god here. Say my name' vibes. He braids her hair. Cat dad. Guaranteed HEA.

The Playlist

Music plays a big part in this author's and these characters lives. If you enjoy some great club bangers, love songs, songs to 'get it on' to, and dash of Canadian hits. This is the playlist for you. Enjoy!

Club Decadent Series Playlist by K.C. Ford

Contents

Chapter One

Addie

The mediator between Addison and her soon-to-be ex slid the divorce papers and a pen toward her. Barry had already scrawled his signature above his printed name, and now it's now her turn. Fucking finally.

Bernard Turner. The name left a bitter taste in her mouth. A smile tipped the corners of her mouth, and relief flooded her system. After today, she never needed to utter it again.

At least he's eager to get this over with. The unending text notifications vibrating on his phone showed Barry needed to get back to his girlfriend, Caroline.

Addie kept her eye roll internal.

Is she bitter that the man who got her pregnant in college and told her he'd be there forever got down and dirty with their neighbor? Not anymore. Barry's her problem now.

Did rage flow through her veins when she came home from work, ill with the flu, desperate to crawl into her own bed to find Barry and their neighbor Caroline going at it like fucking acrobatic rabbits?

Oh, fuck yeah!

Addie realized then that there was no marriage left to fight for when it was more about the bed she longed to crawl into than the man she spent twenty years with.

Thank goodness their daughter Sadie had moved into her dorm a month earlier and missed witnessing the final nail being hammered into the coffin of her parent's relationship.

The nausea Addie fought all morning gave up the battle. She threw up all over them and the sheets they'd fucked on.

Mortified? She supposed she should be. Was she? Hell. No. It's not her mess to clean up anymore.

Addie ignored Barry and Caroline's outrage and the sounds of their retching, wiping her mouth with the back of her hand. Ugh, she needed a shower. She needed to get the fuck out of this house even more.

She locked herself in the bathroom, brushing her teeth and washing her face while they screamed profanities through the door. Addie put on her noise-canceling headphones and packed her bags.

She wheeled her suitcases out the door while Barry and Caroline sputtered and screeched, still covered in vomit.

Addie recovered enough to enjoy the drive by the time her Uber arrived, ready to take her to the hotel she'd booked. Like the mess she left them in, Barry is Caroline's problem now....

The mediator cleared his throat. "We'll need your signature, Mrs. Turner."

"Mrs. Turner?" Addie shifted in her seat and glared at the insipid man.

Everyone at this table knew she never took her husband's last name. Barry being a fucking dick isn't a surprise. Addie clenched her fists in her lap and bit her tongue. Lesson learned, using the guy he recommended because she wanted to get this over with.

She grabbed the pen and tapped the page. The fiery spirit Barry tried to smother for the past twenty years returned a little more each day. "It's Ms. Carter, which you're both more than aware. It even says so right here. Ms. Addison Carter vs. Mr. Bernard Dumb-Fuck-I'm-Glad-He's-Out-Of-My-Life-Cheating-Bastard Turner."

Okay, maybe she's still a little pissed.

Addie met Barry's scowl over the balding head of the mediator, who appeared to be searching for something. Perhaps he searched for cover.

"Oops, must be my copy." She tucked it into her purse when she sensed the incoming insults Barry was about to unleash.

Not this time, and never again.

Addie stood first. "Ah-ah. The ink is dry, and your days of belittling me are done."

The adrenaline kicked in, and she gripped her purse tighter, hiding her shaking hands, wanting out of there.

Addie's steps faltered when the door closed behind her, and tears of relief clouded her vision. She leaned against the wall and took a deep breath. Then she straightened to her full height and shook the last of Barry's influence from her shoulders. She's free, and she's going to make the most of it.

Forty's the new thirty, right? At least, that's what Addie wanted to believe while she waited for her friend to answer the phone.

"Addie," Andrew greeted her, his warm voice a soothing balm on her frazzled nerves. Though she cringed when he said, "You better be calling to tell me your divorce from that piece of shit is final and not to remind me your birthday is next week. We both know I'd never forget."

Addie's deflecting laugh sounded loud and awkward. *Shit.* She meant to call Andrew after she'd signed the papers. In the end, she checked out of society and published her first novel to meteoric success.

Double shit. Addie didn't tell them about that either. She needed to talk to her friends more often and vowed not to leave such gaps between calls or get-togethers.

"*Oh, em gee*, I'm a terrible friend. We finalized the divorce a while ago. Sorry, I didn't realize how much time had passed since we last spoke. With everything I needed to do, I-"

"Addie, you don't need to explain. Tell me you're okay."

Addie settled onto her couch with her phone pressed to her ear. "Yeah, I am. Best in years."

"Well, tell me, what's going on with you? FYI, you'll have to repeat it all when Angela calls you back," Andrew said in an exaggerated whisper. "Her mouth's occupied, or she'd say hello."

Her mouth's what?

"Oh, for fuck's sake. It's the middle of the afternoon, Drew."

"You called me."

"You answered the phone."

Addie pulled the phone away from her ear, and Andrew's laughter filled her apartment. "She's eating lunch. Get your mind out of the gutter, Carter."

"You're such an asshole," she grumbled with a smile.

"That moniker belongs to your ex-husband, plus I can hear you smiling."

Ugh, the man knew her too well.

The silence stretched between them until Andrew asked, "What's going on, Addie?"

She took a deep breath. Of course, Andrew knew there was an ulterior motive for her afternoon call. "I need a favor."

"Anything. Except for making Barry disappear. I draw the line at murder – even for you. I will, however, be happy to make his life miserable."

"No murder." She laughed. "No life difficulties necessary, either. Last I heard, Barry has his hands full with a mess of his creation."

"Fine. If Barry's out of your life, I'll leave him be. What can I do for you?"

Here goes.

She took a deep breath and asked, "Remember the writing I used to do?"

"Yeah. Didn't you minor in creative writing? I always believed you'd become a writer. I remember asking you about it when I saw you on Sadie's first birthday. It saddened me when you mentioned you stopped."

"Life got in the way. What with work, a new baby, and a husband." She ignored Andrew's grunt. Addie knew he blamed Barry for making her give up on her dreams.

The thing is, she gave up on herself, too.

"When things ended, and I moved into my apartment, I found an old box of notebooks filled with my stories. In a true *fuck-it* moment, I revised one and sent it out for submissions. It landed me an agent and a publishing contract."

"Fuck, that's fantastic, Addison. I'm glad you followed your dreams. Are you still teaching?"

"Nope. I finished the semester, and by summer break, a post about my book went viral, which boosted my sales enough to give notice and pursue this author thing full time."

"I'm proud of you, Addie."

"Thanks. Success in this business is based on a lot of luck."

"I know you're talented, Addison. Your growing success is more than just luck."

"Thanks, Drew. I needed to hear that."

Silence fell between them until Andrew asked, "So, what's the favor? Need me to read something you wrote?"

Addie blanched. Fuck no.

If Andrew had read The Professor's Naughty Student, he'd know immediately that Addie based it on the professor she'd crushed on during her first semester of university. He'd never let it go.

Plus, being close friends with him and his wife Angela meant she held intimate knowledge of what went on in their relationship, and reading her WIP in its current state isn't an option either.

"Oh God, please, no." She needed some hands-on research first, which is the root of the favor she required from Andrew.

Andrew chuckled. "Okay... on the one hand, it doesn't surprise me. On the other hand , I can't believe you still won't let me read your stories after all our years of friendship."

"I mean, maybe once this one's finished. This favor is for research. I need a guest pass to Decadent."

"Research? At Decadent?" Addie heard him get up and pictured Andrew pacing while he considered her request.

After the longest minute of her life, he said, "I suspected your stories leaned toward the erotic, and I've perused your overflowing bookshelves on more than one occasion."

"You knew?"

"We're friends. Of course, I did."

She didn't want him to regret his agreement and said, "I appreciate how you always remained honest and open with me, and while your relationship fascinates me, it's not...." Addie searched for the right way to say it.

"It's not what you desire for yourself or your fictional characters?" Andrew finished for her.

"Yeah, kind of...."

Andrew chuckled. "Addison, I know you're not yucking our yum. Everyone has different wants and desires, and finding a partner with the same is like finding a needle in a haystack. I'm glad you know what your limits are. It means you have boundaries around what you do and don't want to try."

"My editor suggested adding more realism and depth to my current novel."

"And you believe you'll gain this depth and realism by visiting a BDSM club?"

"Um, it's what I'm hoping for. I know passes are expensive, and I hoped you'd be able to pull some strings and get me a discount because you're tight with the owner."

"It's not about the money or pulling strings. If I asked Jasper, he'd have a pass delivered to your front door within the next couple of hours. I want to know if going to the club is right for you. I mean, why not draw from your imagination?"

"Fantasy supplemented my entire sex life with Barry. This is a new beginning for me. I want to experience something more intense and real."

"I get it, Addie, and you deserve to experience what you want. Angela and I would never kink shame you or anyone."

"Thanks for understanding, Drew. It's why I came to you. I know you'd never judge me."

Addie sighed; showing vulnerability is never easy. "I'm forty next week, and I've put everyone's needs ahead of mine. For once, I want to experience something exciting and new. This is for me. The cherry on top is the added inspiration for my characters. Will you help me?"

"You know I will. One question. Do Angela and I get to read this book when it's published?"

"If you do, don't tell me."

Andrew laughed. "Addie, you'll need to work on your confidence if you're serious about this."

She sighed. "I know."

love?

Two hours later, someone knocked on her door.

Addie peered through her peephole and recognized the tall, muscular man with auburn hair and a beard standing at her door, thanks to her research into Club Decadent.

She didn't say more than a hello when he held out an envelope and said, "Andrew asked me to give this to you."

"In person?"

When your best friend is friends with the owner of New York's most notorious sex club, the idea of a personal delivery never crossed Addie's mind, yet it's weirdly unsurprising.

He lowered his mirrored sunglasses, and his hazel eyes dazzled her. "Jasper Jones, at your service," he said. His deep voice was rough and right up her alley, yet it did nothing for her.

Huh.

She replaced the envelope he held out with her hand. "Addison Carter. Nice to meet you."

Addison admired his broad shoulders and rugged good looks. The lack of electricity when his large hand wrapped around hers didn't surprise her. Jasper emitted undefineddistinct 'I'm taken' vibes.

"Do you mind if I come in? There are a few things I'd like to discuss with you that are not suited for your public hallway."

Addie stepped back and let him inside.

CHAPTER TWO

Addie

"Nice place you got here," Jasper said.

A guy who owned prime real estate in New York lived in far finer digs than her shoebox-sized apartment. His sheer bulk and height crowded her space, making her apartment seem microscopic.

Yikes, her laundry is all over the couch.

She shoved her folded clothes into the basket and threw it on her unmade bed. Addie shut her bedroom door and offered Jasper a seat on the couch she'd cleared.

"I'm about to indulge in coffee number three. Can I get you one? It's nothing fancy. Dark roast with vanilla oat milk."

"Sounds perfect, thank you."

Addie returned from her kitchenette with their steaming cups and found Jasper studying the photos on the end table.

"My daughter Sadie on the day I dropped her off at university," she said, setting their coffees down.

Jasper studied the picture and then her. His assessing gaze ghosted over her from the top of her head to the tips of her toes.

"The purple suits you," Jasper complimented. Her mousy brown hair was one of many changes Addie made when she kicked Barry out of her life for good. Besides, she rocked these gorgeous purple locks.

"Thanks. It's part of my new rebellion phase."

"Well, rebel looks good on you." Jasper looked at the picture of her and her daughter again, a wistful smile on his face. "Reminds me of when I took my sister to campus for the first time."

Addie knew she'd ventured into sensitive territory, yet Jasper seemed open to her curiosity when she asked, "You must be close."

He picked up his own mug and took a sip. "This is excellent, by the way."

"Thanks."

When Jasper met her gaze, sadness lingered in his. "Despite being twelve years younger, my sister and I are very close. I became her guardian when our parents passed away."

"I'm sorry for your loss. It's good you had each other."

"I'm glad we did too. I'd returned from a harrowing mission, and with Joanna still in her last year of high school, I resigned from the service and received an honorary discharge. Decadent came after I sent her off to university. Now she's a mom, and I'm a proud uncle."

"Oh, wow. Congrats."

"Our mom would've loved being a nana." Jasper stared into the depths of his mug. She sensed he didn't share often.

"Hope you aren't looking for classified information, or I may be in trouble. You're easy to talk to," Jasper said, confirming Addie's suspicions.

It's not the first time she'd heard it. "I am easy to talk to. FYI, I'm also a vault. All classified secrets are safe with me." Addie mimed locking her lips and throwing away the key.

Jasper chuckled. "Good to know." He set his empty cup back on the table and tapped the envelope she left there, ready to give her the lowdown, she guessed.

"The paperwork required for our files is in here, along with the guest pass. Fill it out and bring it with you. They won't admit otherwise."

"Okay. I'll go over it this week and have it filled out by Friday."

"Andrew mentioned it's a special day, and on a Friday the 13th, no less. More than a few individuals will do their kinky version of Jason."

Addie rolled her eyes. Leave it to Andrew to twist all her monumental events into one. "Yeah, it'll be fun to celebrate my fortieth while popping my 'going to a sex club for the first time' cherry and tempting the fates by doing it all on a Friday the 13th."

Addie focused on the chipped polish on her thumb. "Several months ago, I divorced a man who spent almost our entire marriage criticizing and shunning what I desired. After I caught him cheating...." She met Jasper's intense gaze. "Well, I don't want to wait any longer to discover what I want."

"Addison, I don't believe I'm exaggerating when I say your ex sounds like an asshole."

"He is."

"Being kink-shamed is never easy, and you've no reason to be embarrassed for your curiosity or explore more than what he provided."

Jasper shifted in his seat. "Andrew also mentioned this night is for book research. I don't know if he told you we have rigorous policies regarding our member's privacy."

"What? Oh, no, I'd never violate someone's privacy."

"You must understand why I ask."

"Yes, of course. Beyond my curiosity to explore my desires, this is character research."

Addie removed the polish from two more nails with her nervous fidgeting. Then she ran through her mental calendar, now needing to treat herself to a pre-birthday mani-pedi.

"I-" Addie didn't know why it bothered her; this would be a way to improve her book. Her story will benefit from this kind of experience.

"My editor mentioned my characters need more realism and depth. She wants authenticity. The smell, sound, taste...um, you get my meaning."

Jasper sat forward with a smirk on his lips. "Yeah, I get what you're saying. You want to experience things from the perspective of your characters."

"Yes. It'd be helpful if you'd show me around the club and explain some of the equipment and public scenes if I have questions."

Jasper winced. "I can't. I have this-"

Addie jumped in with a preemptive apology. "Oh, my goodness, I'm sorry. I didn't mean to put you on the spot. You're a busy man who doesn't have time to coddle-"

"Addison, stop." Jasper's command halted her mid-sentence. She got the sense that he never needed to repeat himself.

He cleared his throat and sat back. "Sorry, I didn't mean to interrupt. You've got it wrong. I'd be happy to show you around. It's a prior engagement that'll keep me from the club Friday night."

"Oh, okay. No problem. I can check out the place on my own. Maybe meet someone interested in showing me the ropes. Ha-ha. Maybe not actual ropes, though I've always wanted to know what it'd be like to be tied up...."

"Addison?" Amusement laced his voice when he got her attention. "How about I have one of my Dungeon Masters show you around?"

"Then what? Are we in for a game of D&D?" she snickered. "Kidding."

"Hilarious." When his laughter subsided, Jasper said, "In all seriousness, though, the DMs are vital to everyone's safety."

Jasper gave her an assessing look and said, "I'll ask Grayson to show you around. He's one of the other owners."

"How many owners are there?"

"There's eight of us. Myself, Xander, Taylor, Jonathan, Gray, West, Everly, and Reign. We met and bonded for life in the same military squad. When I put in my papers, they did, too."

Jasper chuckled. "We've always maintained an all-for-one and one-for-all mentality. After I got my sister situated, I focused on opening Decadent, and when I did, I gave them each a five percent stake and lifetime memberships. Except for Grayson, he insisted on buying in and owns twenty percent. He helps run the place."

"Sounds like you're all close and have similar tastes." Addison blushed, and Jasper snorted, hiding it behind a cough.

"In the world of BDSM, no two kinky people are alike. I can promise you, Grayson is a good man who'll keep you safe and show you around. I'll add it to his calendar and email him your details. The hostess at the reception desk will alert him when you arrive."

Addie sat there in stunned silence.

Jasper cleared his throat. "Did you have questions?"

Addie didn't know what to ask first, as so many things swirled about her head. "None come to mind. The moment you walk out the door, I'm sure I'll come up with at least a dozen," Addie said.

"Funny how our minds work, huh?"

"For me? It's the standard."

Jasper chuckled. "I left my business card in the envelope. You can email me anytime with those questions. I need to get going and pick out a baby gift."

"Oh, fun. Do you know what your sister's having?"

Jasper's smile softened into that of an infatuated uncle when he said, "Yeah. My niece will be here soon."

"Aw...baby girls are such a joy."

"Any suggestions of what to get her will help."

"It's crazy to wrap my head around two decades passing since I've needed any baby-related items. I'd suggest an enormous basket of all those things a new parent can run out of and doesn't have time to get. Things like extra diapers, wipes, blankets, onesies, and socks."

"I remember when Sadie spit up on her last clean outfit. Barry didn't know the washer from the oven and didn't bother to do laundry. Thank goodness my mom arrived with a care package. Motherhood can be overwhelming, yet all the wonderful, sweet moments make the hard ones worth it."

"Hmm. Maybe I'll set Joanna up with a service to keep her supplied with whatever she needs."

"Excellent idea. Your sister will appreciate it. Maybe show up to the party with a special stuffy from Uncle Jasper." She advised, walking him to her door.

"Will do." He stepped into the hall while Addie leaned against her open door. "Pleasure to meet you, Addison."

"You too."

"If you have questions about the paperwork, email me."

"Promise. Have fun on Friday night."

"You do the same," he said, giving her a wink and wishing her a "Happy birthday." Jasper smiled and then disappeared down the stairs.

Addie felt like she'd passed some sort of test or something. Jasper certainly had an interesting way of vetting people.

Chapter Three

Addie

The paperwork proved very in-depth, and it took Addie a few days to complete it and the required background check. On Friday night, she arrived at the club with the completed forms, a page of notes, and her guest pass. All crammed into her clutch.

Addie wiped her clammy palms on her pants, waiting for the doorman to check her identification. The line moved, and she soon handed her coat to the silent person behind the counter, who waved her toward the guest check-in.

While Addie waited her turn, she checked her phone and found a text from Angela.

> **Angela: Happy birthday, bestie. Be open to the possibilities.**

Addie smiled and shut her phone off. She tugged at the deep V of her shirt, walking the fine line between displaying her ample cleavage and not wanting her tits to fall out of her top.

She didn't know what to wear tonight, choosing to play it safe with an all-black ensemble of bum-hugging slacks, a sleeveless wrap top, her best push-up bra, and a pair of knee-high boots with a modest heel to finish the look.

Addie left her hair loose, flowing in soft lavender waves over her shoulders. Though she struggled with being overdressed or underdressed. The people heading into the club wore sexy leather, pleather, and latex to...almost nothing at all.

Wow, Jasper wasn't kidding.

Addie spotted two individuals with a unique spin on Jason in the lobby alone. One wore the infamous white mask with a tuxedo covering their broad shoulders, while the other paired the mask with a leather thong and not much else.

Maybe she should've worn a mask or come on their masquerade night. It might've helped disguise her inexperience and insecurities.

More like the mask will hide her age.

Is she out of her mind for demanding and taking a second chance at forty?

Is a sex club the way to go about it? Will anyone even find her desirable?

"Enough," she muttered. Barry made her feel like shit more times than she can count. She didn't need to do it to herself. Addie tried a different approach and gave herself an inner pep talk.

You're confident and sexy. This is the best you've felt in years. And you're lucky enough to pursue your passion. How many people get to say that? And damn it, you have wants and desires you're allowed to explore.

"Damn right, I do." The hostess's eyes widened, having caught Addie talking to herself.

Addie handed over her pass and paperwork while a blush rose from her throat to her cheeks. "Sorry. The inner pep talk went a little off the rails there."

"No worries. You aren't the first nervous newcomer to walk through our doors. Welcome to Decadent," the woman said, giving Addie a warm smile.

Then she explained how they'd add Addie's information to their secure system and return the papers to her when she was ready to leave.

"We like to reassure everyone of the importance of their privacy and safety. At the end of the night, your guest pass returns to us. If you become a member, you'll get a permanent one." She explained, then she held three wristbands in front of Addie.

"A red band signifies you are off limits, and no one will approach you. We recommend all first-time guests choose a red band to ensure they don't become overwhelmed. You are welcome to select yellow or green. Yellow is open to approach, and green means... well, you're open to all offers. It doesn't mean you have to accept any of them."

Addie considered her choices. She wanted to do some research, which involved being able to meet people and ask questions, and she also wanted something for her. "What if I wear a red band and want to approach someone?"

"You're free to approach someone wearing a green band or... oh, sorry, our system is a little slow tonight. There's a note on your file. I'm to contact Master M when you arrive."

"Yeah, um, sorry. Jasper arranged for someone to meet me and give me a tour."

She picked up the phone and said, "Page Master M, tell him Addison Carter is waiting by guest services."

When she hung up, Addie asked, "Page? Like a lost child in a department store?"

The hostess gave her an indulgent smile. "Not quite. The no cell phone rule extends to the staff. We have in-house phones without cameras to keep us connected. Our 90s-loving boss likes to call them pagers," she said, with a roll of her eyes.

"Master M should be here soon. Please store your belongings and clothing you don't want in the chill lounge down the hall to my right. The FOB on your wristband controls the lock, and locker 275 is yours for the evening."

Addie thanked her and moved to the side to allow the next guest to check-in. She walked the short corridor leading to a luxurious lounge with recessed lighting, velvet couches, changing areas, washrooms, and even a tiny shop with fetish gear.

Not even inside the actual club, it amazed Addie what amenities the place offered. She eyed the shop, and the mannequin displayed in the blue latex catsuit.

Did she dare?

Addie contemplated purchasing a sexier outfit when a sultry and feminine British accent caught her attention. "First time?"

Addie turned to find out who the lyrical voice belonged to and came face-to-face with an attractive woman of indeterminate age.

She rocked a silver pixie cut, and her glasses framed big blue eyes. Her face appeared smooth and lined with life experiences at the same time.

The woman caught sight of the red band on her wrist and stepped back. "Please forgive me. I didn't mean to enter your personal space without consent."

Addie knew the woman meant no harm. "It's fine, and no need to apologize. I'd ask how you guessed, yet I'm pretty sure a neon sign is flashing above my head, announcing it."

"Not quite, dear. I'm Martha," she said, shaking her hand and glancing again at Addie's red wristband.

Right. The signs are everywhere.

"Addie. Nice to meet you." She looked Martha over, taking in her outfit of leather pants and a blood-red corset, the color matching the frames of her glasses.

The woman possessed style and flair, and Addie liked her right away. "While I may be a novice, Martha, I'm guessing you know a bit about this place."

"I do," she said with an honest-to-goodness twinkle in her eye. "You are talking to the interior designer."

"Oh, wow. From what I've seen, the place is something else."

"Honey, wait till you enter the belly of the club."

Addie's excitement eclipsed her nervousness. She wanted to get in there and explore. "What's something a newbie like me should see?"

"Mm...the stories I could tell." She winked. "In a place like this, curious is the best thing to be. The private rooms are all unique, each having a specific theme, and come equipped with many fun and wicked items to use."

"Um...I don't believe I'll use any private rooms this evening. Maybe I'll consider checking one out next time. If there is a next time."

"Oh darling, I've excellent intuition, and I know this won't be your last time here. Besides, there are many other things around the main bar that are guaranteed to titillate you. I can give you a tour if you like."

"Oh, um, I already have it taken care of, thanks. Can you tell me where the lockers are?"

"They're around the corner over there," Martha said, pointing in that direction. "Pleasure meeting you, Addie. I hope you enjoy your time at Decadent."

"Thanks. Have a good night." Addie rounded the corner, found her locker, and stowed her belongings. Then she took a few fortifying breaths and returned to the lobby, hoping she hadn't kept Grayson waiting.

The woman who checked her in snagged Addie's attention when she entered the lobby. "Addison? I apologize. Master M hasn't arrived yet. I'm going to send him another message."

"Did he get tied up?"

Addie clued in to how her question sounded when the hostess snorted with laughter. She leaned closer and confided, "He's not the kind who gets tied up. He's the one who does the tying." She bit her lip and knew the blush she'd calmed earlier covered her cheeks. "Sorry, I meant busy. Anyway, showing me around is a favor to Jasper. Can you message Master M to meet me inside if he has the time? I'm comfortable enough to go in on my own."

The woman gave her an assessing look. "Alright. Through those doors there," she directed to the ones guarded by security.

"You'll go down a short hallway and arrive at the first of three bars. This one is the overlook and boasts views of the dance floor and main stage. You can observe everything from there or go down to the main floor. The cocktail lounge is at the back of the club, and the private rooms are above it."

"Wait, how will uh...Master M find me?"

"Oh, he'll find you. I'm sure he won't keep you waiting much longer. Remember, if you need anything, or if it all gets too much, you can come back here or speak to any of the staff on duty."

"Thanks."

Addie moved past the guard, and when the door closed behind her, the pulsing beat of a classic Biggie song put a wiggle in her hips and a bounce in her step as she made her way inside.

CHAPTER FOUR

Addie

The overlook is like its name implies. A bar sat to her left with a few well-placed high-top tables and two clusters of wingback chairs. Thoughts of a drink and sitting on the supple leather chairs disappeared. The glass railing framing the area, giving everyone an unobstructed view of what's happening below, made Addie catch her breath.

She claimed the spot a couple vacated and tried to look at everything.

Addie rocked her hips to the beat. It's the music she used to dance the night away to, and while she'd never regret the birth of her daughter, the music reminded her of the times she used to flirt, dance, and be free.

It's an odd feeling to be twenty years older and wiser with those freedoms ahead of her again.

The people on the dance floor writhed and rocked together. The main stage rose behind it, separated by a pass-through and a seating area with oversized club chairs and couches. Perfect for getting up close to the stage performances while letting those dancing enjoy too.

Addie wanted closer. She considered getting a drink from the bar to give Grayson a few more minutes to find her, but ultimately, she decided against the alcohol. Better to keep a clear head.

When five more minutes passed, and no one approached her, Addie decided to heck with it. She didn't want to wait any longer and descended the stairs.

Her gaze jumped from those using the stations lining the far wall to the dancers, to the acts on the stage, and back again. Overstimulated, Addie's breathing quickened, and desire flooded her core, dampening her underwear.

Addie scanned the people clinging to one another, grinding and rocking against each other, becoming an extension of the scenes playing out on stage and nearby equipment, and it made her long for something more.

Sometimes being without a partner sucked.

Doubt filled her. Did she make a mistake in divorcing Barry? The idea left a sour taste in her mouth. She'd never be desperate enough to want him back. Right?

Addie spun with the sudden urge to escape and smacked into a wall.

A wall made of man-muscle.

Her head landed beneath his chin, and her nose pressed against the base of his throat. Addie's lungs filled with spice and leather, and she may have muttered something like, "Wow, you smell amazing." Which she'd neither confirm nor deny.

The desire to keep her nose pressed to his skin intensified. Yet, the rational portion of Addie's brain got it together.

No matter what Addie felt. This man was a stranger; she needed to extract herself from his personal space.

When she tried to step back, his large hands gripped her biceps, keeping her close. Addie tilted her head back, an apology on the tip of her tongue when she met his dark eyes.

Eyes dark enough, they absorbed the light and peered into her soul. Zing. Oh, wow. Oh... oh, no.

Damn. Why did Addie have the sudden urge to zag the moment she zinged?

She'd collided with the hottest guy she's ever laid eyes on. Short brown hair, a powerful jaw, full lips, and shoulders broad enough to block everyone else out. Damn, his obsidian eyes held her captive while he studied her right back.

Addie held her breath and waited for the inevitable rejection.

Men who looked like sex on a stick don't go for women like her – mother to a nineteen-year-old, divorced, carrying a bit of extra junk in her trunk. Perhaps going through a mid-life crisis – oh, it's more than, perhaps.

Still, his expression showed interest, and his magnetic eyes shimmered with heat.

He must be at least ten years younger than she is. It seemed like everyone here was. Despite being the furthest thing from the truth, impostor syndrome sunk its claws into her. If this wall of male perfection making all her lady parts zing didn't block her way, she'd already be running.

"I-"

"Are you alright?" His voice rumbled, the sound coming from deep within his chest.

Did she moan?

His brow furrowed, and his expression turned to one of concern.

Yup. Moaned.

Christ, he's beautiful.

Snap out of it, Addie.

"I gotta go. Sorry about walking into your space...or maybe you stood in mine?"

Did she make a squeaky sound there at the end? Oh, god.

Addie stepped back, and he let her go despite his apparent concern. It's when she got an entire look at all she'd plastered herself against.

His leather vest has a fluorescent patch with the letters DM stitched on it.

Is this Master M? Grayson? What did she call him?

Panic made its way into her system. Jasper isn't sadistic enough to select a sex god to show her the ins and outs of this place, is he?

Oh, fuck. Jasper is.

The leather vest did nothing to hide the chest harness he wore beneath, emphasizing his sculpted pecs, cut abs, and tattoos. One spanned his chest from shoulder to shoulder below his collarbone. The leather straps obscured the words, making reading impossible in the muted club lighting.

Damn, *Addie wanted to know what it said.*

Her gaze dipped further to find leather pants molded to his lower body, emphasizing his powerful legs and what hung between. *Oh, fuck. The man has muscles on top of muscles, among... other generous attributes.* And a pair of well-worn Doc Martens completed his sexy-as-fuck look.

When the realization hit, it hit like a frying pan to the back of the head. The physical manifestation of the MMC in her current manuscript stood in front of Addie.

The one she's here to research.

How's this possible?

Except this guy has an affinity for leather – though she may add it to her character's repertoire.

Addie shook her head, trying to clear her vision, and when the sex god came into focus, she blurted, "My goodness, you need to come with a warning."

Ugh, why *did she say that?*

His expression shifted to amusement, and Addie forgot everything, even her next breath when he graced her with a dentist's dream smile.

Sweet baby Jesus. Houston? We have dimples.

The sights, the sounds, the man... *oh,* God, *the man...* the entire combination put Addie in a sensory overload. She needed to leave, or she might combust at any moment.

Addie glanced behind her, backing away, putting space between her and the person she knew would deliver every fantasy she ever desired on a silver platter.

Wait. Why is she running away?

She gave *Mr. Tall, Dark, and Sexy* one last look, noting every detail about him. The man she pictured in her mind exists beyond the pages of her manuscript, and it's freaking her the fuck out.

Did she conjure him?

Oh, sure, and maybe her laptop became possessed. Now, there's a story idea. Oh my god, stop it.

She'd make a note to explore the concept further.

Other people have literal, full-on internal conversations, right?

Right?

He stepped toward her, asking her to wait. Addie pretended not to hear him and made a beeline for the stairs. Once she reached the landing, she peered back for one last look. Someone halted his pursuit, and disappointment filled her at her unhindered escape.

Addie retrieved her stuff from her locker, ready to hightail it out of there, when she remembered she needed to give them the guest pass and get her paperwork back.

A different girl stood behind the counter and retrieved the forms. Addie shoved them in her purse, not realizing she dropped a folded sheet on her way out the door.

The twenty-minute cab ride dragged, and Addie sighed with relief when the cabbie dropped her off at her building.

She climbed the four flights, and with a few steps left to her apartment door, wet, squishy noises beneath her feet alerted her that something was very wrong. The faded red carpet looked a lot darker, and when she reached her door, she heard the distinct sound of water cascading inside her place.

What the fuck?

"Oh, no. No, no, no, no," Addie chanted. Praying it's not what it is. She fumbled with her keys and unlocked her door, and when Addie swung it wide, she found a shower in her entryway.

She ducked around the waterfall, trying and failing not to get soaked. A puddle crossed her living room floor, heading toward her bedroom and writing nook.

"Oh, shit fuck, my laptop." Addie made a mad dash for her room and found everything still dry while the water quickly encroached.

Back in the living room, Addie unplugged her TV and sound system, but the bottoms of the speakers were already soggy. She lifted those on her kitchen counter and cursed every second the water poured into her living space.

One of her neighbors came out of their apartment to investigate the noise, or maybe the water entered their place, too. Addie needed the building manager to shut off the water and searched for his number in her contacts.

Mrs. Lewis, her nosy neighbor, appeared in her doorway. "Is this your doing?" she asked.

"No, Ma'am, I arrived home a few minutes ago to find it like this."

"Do something about it. You don't want it spreading to other apartments. I have a lot of irreplaceables, you know."

Addie tried not to let Mrs. Lewis faze her. Her neighbor may be old and curt. She's also quiet and keeps to herself. Unless her *irreplaceables* are at risk.

"Calling the super right now, Mrs. Lewis," she said, placing the ringing phone to her ear. Addie planned to march downstairs and bang on his door if he didn't answer in the next two seconds.

"This better be good." The half-asleep man grumbled in her ear. Well, he's in for a rude awakening.

"This is Addison Carter in 4B. There's a burst pipe in the apartment above mine, and water is flooding my place and down the hall. I'm sure several angry phone calls will come your way in moments if you don't turn the building's water off and get a plumber over here ASAP."

"Shit. Alright, I'm on my way." He hung up on her, not allowing anything else to be said.

Asshole.

"He's taking care of it now, Mrs. Lewis. The water will be off soon."

"It better be fixed by the time I need to wash and set my curls," she huffed, returning to her apartment.

"Sure thing, Mrs. Lewis. I'll get right on it." Addie blew an exasperated breath, moving her things out of the water and saving most of her belongings from getting damaged.

"Happy fucking birthday to me." She looked at the mess of her apartment, and the water pressure trickled to nothing.

"At least it's shut off. I can't stay in this fucking mess, though." She never meant for this apartment to be long term, moving into it when she separated from Barry. It's beyond the time she looked for something else.

Addie needed to put a positive spin on this waterlogged situation. Otherwise, she might sit on the wet floor and cry over how shitty her birthday turned out.

It's time she invested the savings she squirreled away in purchasing a forever home. A little acreage outside the city with a forest view from her writing room window.

"Fuck it. I'm booking a bougie hotel room for the weekend." She'd deal with finding a short-term rental next week.

Tomorrow, when she met her besties, Angela and Andrew, for her birthday dinner, Addie planned to ask them if they could put her in touch with a real estate agent who'd work a miracle to find her a home asap.

Armed with a plan, the adrenaline Addie rode until this moment dissipated. The late hour meant exhaustion weighed her down, and tears pricked her eyes.

All she wanted to do was eat the birthday cupcake her daughter Sadie sent her and relive every second of her short yet eventful visit to a sex club. She won't be doing any of that tonight.

Addie needed to find a hotel, pack some things, and try to get some sleep. Then she'll face what to do about her living situation and the rest of her belongings tomorrow.

Sleep eluded Addison when she collapsed into the hotel room bed in the wee hours of the morning.

Dark magnetic eyes, a chiseled jaw, and full lips caused her thighs to clench and for her to mutter a string of curses while she tossed and turned, finally giving in to the need to get herself off.

Addie got up and searched each bag she brought. Discovering her vibrator wasn't one of the essential items she packed.

"Are you fucking kidding me?"

She groaned in frustration and starfished in the center of the mattress, staring at the ceiling, deciding now was as good a time as any to have a chat with the universe.

"Um, I'm confused about how this whole karma thing works. In case you forgot, Barry did the cheating. Forty's supposed to be something fabulous for me, and now you've got me questioning all my recent decisions."

No answer came, though, as her eyelids grew heavy, and exhaustion won out.

Chapter Five

Gray

Gray kept his gaze riveted on the submissive cuffed to the chains hanging above them. Their feet on the concrete floor squeezed the wood block between them, keeping their legs spread and giving them a place to send the energy absorbed from each strike.

They moaned long and low, showing no sign their cane-wielding dominant caused any discomfort.

Last week, the couple approached Gray and asked for help with a scene, wanting a second set of eyes to observe their partner while they remained focused on their task.

"I'm Jax, and this is Piper," they said, introducing themselves when they discussed what they'd need from Gray.

Piper possessed a high pain tolerance, and they'd asked Jax for more, never uttering their safeword until Jax made the call and did.

Jax worried if they didn't give Piper what they needed, they might go elsewhere to someone who didn't have their utmost safety in mind.

It's not the first time Gray monitored a scene in one of the club's private rooms and agreed to help.

While some of the private rooms offered viewing decks for voyeurs and exhibitionists, who wanted more intimacy than the main stage provided. Other rooms allowed for privacy, no matter the number of guests.

The dungeon boasted authenticity, except for its lack of location in the bowels of an ancient castle. Stone floors, shackles, stocks, and many other torturous devices found in a masochist's and sadist's wet dreams are here in this room.

Even the temperature is chillier than anywhere else, enhancing the ambiance. Not for the first time, Gray wished he wore a Henley under his vest and not his favorite leather harness.

Gray's back pocket vibrated with a message. Whoever needs him can wait or contact one of the other DMs on duty.

He didn't work Friday nights often and planned to monitor this scene, then find a willing sub for the night. His plans got upended because Jasper needed him to cover for him tonight.

Jasper's sister Joanna is having her baby shower tonight, and her brother's attendance is mandatory. While Gray might've ribbed him about having to play the diaper game, Jasper's sister is special to all of them. After all her struggles, she and her husband, Jonathan, deserved this happiness.

Gray focused on the two people in front of him. Jax held the cane with such confidence. For each implement they used, leading to this one, they handled it with care and precision.

The thwack of the cane reached his ears, and Piper's head lulled between their chained arms. Gray believed Piper had reached their unreachable limit.

Gray shifted his stance. The ache in his leg intensified from standing in the same spot for too long. His subtle movements gained Jax's attention, and with a tilt of his chin, he signaled Jax to stop.

Jax dropped the cane and took a moment to admire the marks each implement created. The gentle touch stirred Piper from their blissed-out state.

Gray admired their skill. Jax inflicted the maximum amount of pain while never breaking Piper's skin. Those welts will linger, turning into black and blue bruises until they become faded memories, and Jax gifted Piper another set.

"You look perfect, my love," they praised.

Their connection and Jax's skill assured Gray they fulfilled Piper's needs without taking things too far. Jax caught Grayson's attention and mouthed, 'Thank you.' Then, they gave their complete focus to Piper.

"I have peace." Piper sobbed into the crook of Jax's neck.

"I know, pet, I'll always strive to get you there. After tonight, I know I can."

Gray closed the door on their conversation and stepped into the anteroom, which buffered the dungeon from the rest of the club.

He welcomed the rise in temperature when the buzzing in his pants pocket went off a second time. Gray checked his messages.

Addison Carter is waiting for you at Guest Services.

Shit. He forgot the other thing he'd promised Jasper he'd do. Show a guest around and answer her questions. It's why he'd told Jax and Piper to meet him earlier.

The monitoring session went longer than expected, and this message came in twenty-five minutes ago. Gray didn't mean to keep a guest waiting this long. Then he read the second message from Kari.

Disregard. Addison Carter is exploring on her own.

"What the fuck?" Gray bypassed the security guard to get to the club's offices. What game is Kari playing? He swiped his fob, stepped into his office, and dialed her extension.

"I'll call off the search party I sent to look for you."

This is how Kari answers his call with sass and a bratty attitude. While brats aren't his thing, he adored this one like an annoying little sister, and Gray couldn't wait to meet the Daddy who nurtured her fiery spirit.

"What do you mean, Addison Carter is exploring alone?" Gray asked, getting right to the point.

"Well, let me break it down for you, caveman. When a woman gets left waiting, sometimes she doesn't want to stick around and wait any longer. Besides, it's not like you left explicit instructions to keep her in the lobby. It's the woman's birthday, for crying out loud. She wanted to get her freak on, not wait for you to give her a tour. She went inside ten minutes ago."

Well, shit, Gray didn't mean to put a damper on the woman's birthday. He'd apologize to Addison when he found her. "Sorry, I didn't check in with you until now."

"S'okay. Gotta go. More guests are arriving." Dial tone met Gray's ear.

He flipped open his tablet to check the system for Addison's paperwork and ID and discovered it hadn't uploaded. "What the fuck is going on tonight?"

He'll chat with the admin department to remind them how vital it is to keep on top of guest information. Gray headed to the main floor to search for Ms. Carter himself. Fuck, he hoped nothing else went wrong tonight.

Gray searched the speakeasy lounge where a few of the regulars congregated. Mistress Eve claimed her usual spot, the throne, in the corner. He jutted his chin toward her in greeting. She's ex-military and a silent partner in this place like the rest of his squad. The lone female on their team and one of the strongest people Gray knew.

He's still alive with nothing more than a bum leg because of her quick actions during their last mission. Everly tipped her chin in return. His sister-in-arms is a bodyguard with Elite Security, the company Xander Ward founded. Though Xander was on an extended assignment overseas, Everly ran the day-to-day operations here. He'd stop to chat, but she was being catered to by one of her puppies, and he needed to find Addison.

When Gray crossed in front of the stage, a hint of sweet vanilla teased his senses, and long, wavy, purple hair caught his eye. It cascaded midway down their back, leading to a set of hips framing the perfect ass. Gray wanted to run his fingers through the strands to see if they felt as soft as they looked. As if pulled by an invisible string, Gray moved closer.

Could this be Addison?

Gray didn't get the chance to ask. The woman turned and planted her face in the center of his chest. He caught her by her arms and steadied her to keep her from stumbling. Her height put her head by his chin, and Gray took a deep breath, confirming she was the source of the sweet vanilla scent.

Then her sultry, feminine voice hit Gray's ears, and her lips moved against the base of his throat. "Wow, you smell fantastic."

He grunted when she breathed him in. Gray didn't begrudge her while he did his damnedest to memorize the nuances of her sweet scent.

She tipped her head back, and he stared into the face of an angel. Gray didn't want to let her go, and when he did, he missed the way she fit against him.

"I-"

"Are you alright?" Gray asked, hoping he hadn't hurt her when she ran into him. She took another step away while her gaze remained locked on his.

Christ, she's beautiful.

The woman was curvy in all the right places. Big tits, pouty lips, and her hair dyed his favorite color. Desire hit him like a Mack truck.

"I've gotta go. Sorry about walking into your space, or maybe you're standing in mine?" Oh no, he made her nervous, and not in the fun, anticipatory way.

"Wait." The somewhat conservative outfit, alone and nervous? This must be Addison. He moved toward her, and she disappeared through a break in the crowd. He made to go after her when Jax and Piper stepped into his path.

"Master M, we wanted to thank you again. This has brought our relationship to a new level. You've given me the confidence to explore my pet's limits."

His eyes tracked the woman until she reached the top of the stairs. Gray caught her gaze when she looked back. Everyone around him fell away until she broke their connection and disappeared beyond the landing.

He turned to Jax and said, "Of course. Please ask if you need me to monitor a scene again. You are beautiful together. Enjoy the rest of your evening."

"We're done for the night and headed out. I prefer to tend my pet in the comfort of our home. Good night, Master M."

Gray smiled and bid them goodnight. He didn't bother trying to catch the woman. He'd confirm if it's Addison. Then he'd figure out how to entice her to return so he could make tonight up to her.

CHAPTER SIX

Gray

"Earth to Grayson."

Gray leaned against the glass railing, oblivious to the staff cleaning the main floor, when Kari waved her hand in front of his face. Absorbed in his musings, he never even heard her approach.

"Sorry, got some stuff on my mind."

"No kidding. I must've said your name five times." Kari turned and struck a pose, a remnant of her modeling days. The height of this woman is intense, and depending on the heels she wears, there are nights she's taller than Gray.

"Is it something or someone who's got you occupied?"

Gray pushed away from the railing. "I'm not in the mood to be your gossip."

"I knew it," she said with triumphant glee.

Damn it.

"No, you don't. It's the discussion I need to have with the admin team. Why can't I access our system or anyone's information?" he deflected.

"Oh, shit. I meant to tell you. There's an issue with the server. The system went down, but it's fixed now."

"Since we're closed now, the info's not helpful. Why didn't you tell me?"

"Jasper called to check in after Joanna's party ended, and when I mentioned it, he said not to bother you with it and to transfer him to the department. With your monitoring session, meeting with Addison, and looking after things, I'm sure he wanted to help and take something off your plate. You know how Jasper is."

"I'm in charge tonight and am supposed to be told about system failures. The system being down is one reason I missed the meeting with Addison."

Kari's eyes widened. "The two of you didn't find one another?"

"No, we didn't. Well, I don't think we did."

"Oh."

"Yeah. Oh."

"What're the other reasons?"

"The monitoring session went longer than expected. And someone didn't keep Addison at guest services, even though there's a note on her file to do so."

"No, there's not."

"What do you mean? I entered it myself."

"It said, and I quote, 'Meeting with Addison Carter.' It didn't say, please keep Addison Carter waiting for an indefinite amount of time in the lobby."

Kari's eye roll finisher will have someone someday pull her over their knee to turn her ass molten red. Today isn't the day.

He growled with frustration and said, "You know what I meant."

"Well, I didn't know your session went long, and when Addison turned her baby-blue eyes on me, asking if she's allowed to meet you inside, I found no reason to refuse her."

Baby-blue?

He wanted to ask if Addison's hair was a shade of purple when he caught sight of the folded paper Kari held. Hard to miss since she kept tapping it against the top of the railing. "What's with the paper?" he asked.

"This?" she asked, waving it under his nose. "Oh, now, this is interesting." Her expression turned mischievous, her lips forming a smirk, and Gray knew her inner brat had taken control.

"I found it on the floor when I returned from my break. Simone covered for me but doesn't know who dropped it."

"And?" He prodded when she paused her story.

"Annnd, I'm not sure. There's a description of a guy who sounds an awful lot like you, something about an innocent heroine...blah, give me a partner who knows what they're doing. Am I right?" She snorted and held the folded sheet out for him to take.

Gray took the page and skimmed it. The description sounded a lot like him.

"I know who wrote this," she said, tapping the corner of the page.

"Why didn't you lead with that info?" He squinted at what seemed to be a watermark in the corner.

"Because this is more fun. Also, it says Copyright A.D. Carter, in case you can't read without your cheaters."

"Are you telling me this belongs to Addison Carter?"

"Well, it seems pretty co-inky dinky. I googled A.D. Carter, and this is the top result." Kari held out her phone, turning the screen toward him to read it.

NOW AVAILABLE ON ALL PLATFORMS:

THE PROFESSOR'S NAUGHTY STUDENT

"What?"

"I know, right?" Kari said, snatching her phone back and not letting him read anymore. "I've already one-clicked it, and it's waiting for me on my Kindle when I get home. Can't wait to dive under the covers and read this bad boy."

"Kari." Gray tried for patience and asked again, "How do you know they're the same person?"

If the word duh has a physical embodiment, it's how Kari looked at him. "Because, Mister Military Ops Guy, they have the same last name. Plus, the initials A.D. sound like an abbreviation for Addie. Full name, Addison Carter. Case solved." She accompanied her declaration with another eye roll.

Gray is such a fool, and Kari's teasing didn't help. "Can you please tell me what Addison looks like?"

"You don't know what she looks like?"

"The system went down, remember?"

His patience thinned while Kari tapped her index finger against her bottom lip. Then she laughed, sending him over the edge.

"What is it?" Gray demanded.

"It makes sense now."

"What does?"

"Jasper is matchmaking again. He asked how you vibed almost when you met. He sounded disappointed when I told him I didn't know. Oh, this is fun. Listen, I've gotta go. There's a book calling my name."

Kari had almost reached the lobby when he recovered from the shock. "Wait, what?" She held the door open and raked her gaze over him.

Full of mischief, she said, "Jasper sure knew what he was doing when he asked you to take care of Addison. Several staff members trained to give someone new a tour, yet the boss man chose you. I'm sure the system's up and running, and you can access Addison's file now. Byeee." She waved as the door closed behind her.

Gray made a beeline for his office and grabbed his tablet. The fatigue hit him, and so did the ache in his leg when he dropped into his chair. Fuck, extra shifts are a bitch when his home's a ninety-minute drive away on a good day.

Gray won't be making the trip home tonight, using the basement apartment at Jasper's like he did whenever he stayed in the city. Though he craved the peace of his farmhouse and workshop.

The farm became his salvation after his injury and subsequent honorary discharge from his military service. It helped him heal inside and out. He missed Minnie too, hoping she'd be okay without him. He always experienced a little anxiety when he left her longer than usual.

The system took time to reboot, and Gray drummed his fingers against his desk while he waited for the tablet to load. When it did, he logged in and located Addison's file.

The goddess with the purple hair stared back at him.

CHAPTER SEVEN

Addie

If this is forty, Addie wanted a do-over.

Her eyelids fluttered, and unfamiliar surroundings came into focus. Her confusion didn't last when the past twenty-four hours rushed through her mind. Addie groaned and buried her head beneath the hotel's too-soft pillows.

Club Decadent.

The real-life manifestation of the character she smelled like her favorite things. Leather, sex, and sin.

The flood that happened in her apartment.

"Oh, fuck, fuckety-fuck-fuck," Addie groaned, adding blankets to the pillows over her head, trying to suffocate the memory or herself. Whichever came first. When she kept breathing, Addie sighed and flung the bedding to the bottom of the bed.

Addie snorted, finding herself overly dramatic.

She needed a shower, a calorie-laced hotel breakfast, to text her daughter with an update on her current living conditions, and to head back to her apartment to assess the damage in the light of day. Then, Addie needed to find something more permanent than a hotel room.

First, coffee and calories. Then she'd deal with everything else.

After her exhausting day, the last thing Addie wanted to do was go out and socialize for a second night. There's no way she can cancel. They're her dearest friends, and her birthday dinner plans with Andrew and Angela are a long-standing tradition. Despite her exhaustion, there's no way she'd miss out on a melt-in-your-mouth fillet or time with her besties.

A hot, steamy shower relaxed Addie's tired muscles, and a café mocha, which may backfire later, re-energized her.

Addie glanced around the cluttered hotel room; she stacked half a dozen bags and suitcases under the table with the TV and eight medium-sized boxes on either side.

Did the hotel staff ask if she planned to extend her stay after several trips from the double-parked car service to her room? Like five times, at least.

The room seemed tiny, with her belongings crammed in every corner. Addie will store the rest until she finds the home she wants to buy.

Andrew must know someone who'd mesh well with her and work to find her dream home. He's her best bet. The man has connections everywhere.

She pulled the dress she wanted to wear from the hanger. Addie bought it for herself when she received her first royalty payment. She'd saved it for a special occasion, and dinner with her favorite people was the perfect time to wear it.

The emerald-green sleeveless cocktail dress hugged her curves, and the color made her eyes pop, making her hair look even more vibrant.

She gathered her waves into a twisted knot, doing her make-up with smoky eyes and a light lip. She added a spritz of her signature scent and grabbed her coat, ready to go.

Addie chose not to grab a cab and walked the four blocks to the restaurant, letting the city's vibrant atmosphere energize her more than her mocha ever could. She arrived moments after Andrew and Angela stepped out of their SUV.

"Happy birthday, darling. You look gorgeous." Angela greeted her with a light kiss on each cheek.

It's high praise coming from the literal angel in front of her. "Thank you. You do too."

Andrew echoed his wife's sentiments, giving her a hug. "You didn't walk from the subway, did you?"

"I promise it's all good. I'm staying at a hotel a few blocks from here."

"Oh? Did you do a birthday hotel-spa weekend?" Angela asked.

"It's a little more complicated. I'll fill you in on the details inside."

"Well, let me get you beautiful ladies to our table, then. Addie must have lots to fill us in on," he said, giving her a knowing look. Andrew placed a hand at the base of Angela's spine and offered Addie his other arm to escort them inside.

The hostess seated them with menus, and the sommelier arrived to discuss wine options. Andrew ordered a Pinot Noir for the table since they planned to have the filet mignon. The sommelier returned with the selection and poured each a glass upon Andrew's approval.

Addie never understood all the hubbub. Andrew always selected something even her meager palate appreciated.

Wine in hand, Andrew raised his glass and said, "A toast to a vibrant, amazing woman whose strength shines from within. Amazing things are happening, Addie. I know it. Happy birthday."

"Yes, happy birthday; celebrating you once a year is never enough. Cheers."

She basked in their praise. "Cheers."

Angela told her the same thing every year, and Addie believed she gave her too much credit for pulling a classic HIMYM move. At the uni pub, she'd slid up to Angela at the bar and asked her if she'd met Andrew. Then she went full *Barney* and left them to their obvious chemistry. The two are just as magnetic today.

The server took their order, leaving them time to chat while they waited for their meals when Angela asked, "If you're not treating yourself to a spa weekend, why are you staying in a hotel?"

Addie raised her glass in salute to the shitshow of the past forty-eight hours and said, "Well. I received a late birthday present when I got home last night." She paused for dramatic effect. "A pipe burst in the ceiling above my entryway."

"Oh, no. Is everything ruined?" Angela asked with concern.

"Why didn't you call us?" Andrew demanded.

"I'm okay, I swear. Got home in time to save almost everything," Addie informed them, then met Andrew's gaze. "I didn't call because of the late hour, and I didn't want to wake you or disrupt your night."

"You can't stay in a hotel until things get fixed. I insist you stay with us." Addie smiled, knowing Andrew meant every word, but she wouldn't be the one to impede their extracurriculars.

Andrew and Angela are... how does one describe friends who bang with the frequency of rabbits, except to say they bang like rabbits?

"And cramp your sexy time? Never in a million years, my friend." She laughed and took a healthy sip of her wine. "This is delicious. Excellent choice, as always."

"Don't change the subject by stating a fact. My excellent taste goes without question," Andrew said, giving Addie a wink and his wife a tender kiss. "You can't stay in a hotel for the foreseeable future."

Addie fiddled with the stem of her wineglass. "I know. The landlord gave me the fantastic news this morning: repairs will take three to four weeks, and I informed him it voided my lease and I'd be moving out."

Addie savored another mouthful of wine. "You know what? This is the push I needed to find my forever home. I have a couple of temporary places to look at tomorrow, and I'm hoping you'll have the name of a real estate agent who can find me what I want."

"Depends. What are you looking for, and where do you want to live?" Their conversation paused when the server arrived with their first course. It gave Addie a moment to picture the wish list she'd added to over the past few months.

"I want a place away from the hustle and bustle of the city, yet still have access to it. An actual house. I haven't lived in a house with a yard since I lived with my parents. Nothing big or fancy, two bedrooms, two bathrooms, and an office space featuring a treelined view. While I don't mind neighbors, I want to pretend I don't have neighbors."

"Something move-in ready, with a few projects to add my flair to the place. While I love the city and its endless energy, I'm eager to find my dream home."

"So, somewhere in northeastern Connecticut? Like the New Haven area?"

"Yes. New Haven's at the top of my list, with Bridgeport a close second, though places there are above my price point. Properties get snatched off the market quickly, and if I find something, I'll need to make an offer right away."

"I don't know any specific agents who handle the area. There's someone I know who lives around New Haven. I can have him contact you? Is email okay? He bought his place there a few years ago."

"I trust your judgment. I'll be on my laptop for the next few days. Email is the best. My phone's turned off while I'm working, anyway."

Their server returned and exchanged their empty salad plates for their main course.

"I'll check if he can help," Andrew said.

"It's all I can ask. I may take a weekend trip there and familiarize myself with the area." Addie sliced through her medium-rare fillet like butter, which melted on her tongue. "Mm...heaven."

"We'll send our compliments to the chef," Angela said, digging into hers.

"I swear the food is more delicious each time we come here." Andrew agreed. Conversation ceased while they enjoyed their meals.

When Addie placed her cutlery across her plate, Andrew asked, "Are you going to tell us how it went at Decadent?"

Her last bite of food caught in her throat, making her cough. She saved face with another generous sip of wine.

Damn, she's going to need more than a glass for this conversation.

"The place lives up to its name." She stalled, hoping to buy some time. "The opulence of the lounge alone...well, I wanted to spend hours there. I mean, there's a fetish store in it."

"They spared no expense with the place. All those nooks and crannies to get frisky in," Angela said with a knowing smirk.

Andrew cleared his throat, sending a look toward his wife. "I'll have to remember all those nooks and crannies the next time we go to the club, Angel."

Her friend melted into a pool of submissive goo whenever Andrew called her angel.

"Did Jasper show you around and answer your questions?" he asked, pushing Addie closer to revealing the moment it all went to shit.

"Jasper has quite the presence, doesn't he?" Angela inquired with a knowing smile.

"It surprised me to find him on my doorstep last week," she replied, side-eyeing her friend.

"He put me at ease. No zing, though I do 100 percent get his Viking-like appeal. Anyway, he didn't work last night and arranged for Grayson to show me around."

"Oh?" "Oh?"

"Why did you both say it like that?"

Andrew cleared his throat. "Jasper may have an ulterior motive."

"Jasper attended a party for his sister. I don't doubt that he had other plans. What's his ulterior motive?"

"Oh, I'm not disputing his plans; it's...." Angela cleared her throat, looked at Andrew, and then met Addie's gaze. "Don't worry, it's nothing untoward. Jasper likes to match people. He's got a real knack for knowing who's best suited. Though he doesn't believe in finding someone for himself."

"Not quite, Angel." Drew raised a brow, and a silent conversation took place between them.

Addie longed for a connection like theirs.

"Right, not our story." Angela nodded and returned to her new assistant matchmaker role. "Isn't Grayson an absolute smoke show?" She caught her husband's pointed stare. "Where is the lie, darling?"

Andrew grunted. "True."

"And?" said Angela with renewed enthusiasm. "If I'd known you wanted to check out what Decadent offers, I might've set you up with him myself."

"Don't get too excited and plan my next wedding – there's no chance of me getting married again."

"Never say never," Andrew muttered a little too loud from behind his glass.

Addison gave him a distasteful look. "I believe one mistake is enough."

"Who says the next one will be a mistake?"

"Anyway...he stood me up, and I didn't stay beyond looking around, getting overwhelmed, and planting my face in the middle of a guy's chest because I ran into him. Then I went home to the flood. It's a night I don't want to repeat. Can a customer service department give me a refund or exchange for my fortieth?"

Angela squeezed her hand. "I'm sorry, sweetie."

Addie smiled. "This dinner with the both of you has made it better by leaps and bounds."

"You didn't get to experience anything the club offered?" Angela asked.

"Mm, not true. I loved the energy and even met the designer, Martha."

"Oh yes, we're familiar with Martha," Angela said, sipping her wine. When she didn't elaborate, Addie decided it was best not to ask further.

"I didn't get to check out any private rooms she designed, though. Each one's special, right?"

"We haven't used them all," Angela said with a quiet laugh. "We have toured them, and I can attest that each is unique."

"Wait, back up. You face-planted in the middle of a man's chest?" Andrew asked, getting a word in between their back and forth.

Addie drained her glass, holding it out for Drew to refill, which he obliged. "I hoped you'd go along with your wife and let me glaze over that part of the story."

"Oh, I planned on circling back," Angela smirked.

Addie sighed in defeat. If anyone understands, it'll be them. "A scene taking place on stage turned me on, and it got to be a bit much being alone and standing amongst the crowd. I wanted to return to the bar upstairs and wait for Grayson. I didn't make it far and walked face-first into a bare, muscular chest. When I leaned back to apologize and met his dark eyes...I...well, I zinged."

"Zinged?" Andrew asked, confusion marring his brow.

"Um, well, yeah. It's something you both inspired. Remember when I introduced you?"

Angela leaned forward in her chair and waved a long, elegant finger between her and her husband. "You're telling us you experienced a first meeting like ours with the man you collided with, and you didn't stay and talk to him?"

"Nope. I zinged, and then I zagged right out the door." She laughed. "I can't believe I did."

"No kidding." Angela took a sip from her glass. "Dark eyes, you say?"

"Yup, the kind a girl gets lost in. Tall, muscular, and bare-chested, which I already mentioned. Tattoos, a chiseled jaw, and full kissable lips." Addie described him , picturing him in her mind.

"I understand why you're pursuing your writing dream," Angela said, fanning herself.

"Yeah, well, here's the crazy part. It's like the character in the book I'm working on came to life. Like someone plucked him from my manuscript and set him in front of me. I kid you not."

"Wow."

"Oh, don't worry. I know how crazy it sounds. It's what made me hightail it out of there."

"Honey, your book boyfriend coming to life isn't the crazy part. The crazy part was when you left."

"You didn't get a name or anything?"

"Nope. He might've worked there. I'm not sure, though." Addie didn't miss their silent exchange. "Do you know who I'm describing?"

"Maybe."

The server arrived with their dessert. Addison's favorite baked Alaska.

Addie silently thanked the server's timing for diverting their discussion to *oohing* and *aching* over the delicious dessert.

"I insist we drop you off on our way home. You're tipsy; the past two days have got to be catching up with you, Addie. It's a terrible combination for making it back to your hotel in one piece," Andrew said, guiding her and his wife to their waiting car.

Kirk held the rear door of the black Escalade open, brokering no argument. Despite the heady buzz of an excellent wine drunk, Addie didn't miss Kirk's heated look over her friends and the subtle glances they returned.

It's not the first time Addie has concluded there's more going on between her friends and the man who handled their security needs.

It's not Addie's business unless they make it so.

The moment Addie's tush touched the buttery leather, she forgot about issuing a protest for the lift back to her hotel, more than ready to call it a night.

They arrived at her hotel in minutes. Kirk assisted her to the curb, and Andrew followed her to the lobby. "Are you sure you're alright? Kirk will keep Angela company, and I can escort you to your room."

"I promise I can get there by myself." Addie smiled because her friend's protectiveness meant a lot. "Thank you for the offer." She knew he'd wait until she texted him she was safe in her room.

"Addie, things have a way of working out how they're supposed to. You'll see." He kissed her cheek and pressed the call button for the elevator. Ever the gentleman, Andrew stayed until the doors closed her inside.

Andrew tucked Angela under his arm, and Kirk settled behind the wheel. "Kirk?"

"Yes, sir?"

"Dial Grayson Matthew's number and put it on speaker."

"Yes, sir."

"Andrew, what are you doing?" Angela asked, tilting her head to meet his gaze.

"Understanding things and perhaps giving our friends one more little push toward their own happy ever after."

"Darling, you're such a romantic. I agree Addie and Gray are an excellent match. You don't think it's too late to call?" Angela asked while it rang through.

"Nope."

"Hello?" Grayson answered a moment later.

"Gray? It's Andrew Thompson."

"Oh, hey, Drew. What can I do for you?"

"It's nothing to do with me. It's about a dear friend of mine. I believe you may know her, Addison Carter."

"Oh?" Andrew and Angela shared a knowing *ah-ha* look at the interest in his voice. Then they heard him mutter, "The missing puzzle piece. Addison is a friend of yours?"

"First, let me ask. Why didn't you give Addison the tour? She said, you never showed."

"Uh, yeah. I was monitoring a scene, and it went longer than expected, and by the time I got to my messages, Addison had gone exploring on her own."

"Didn't you run into her?"

"Do you have spies everywhere?"

"Not everywhere. Angela and I've come from dinner with Addie, where she told us she had met you without realizing she did."

"What do you mean?"

"Something about face-planting against your broad chest? When Addie described the person, we knew she was talking about you. If you'd introduced yourself, I wouldn't have to assist Jasper in his desire to find you a partner."

"I knew it," Gray muttered. "I didn't even know Addison's identity until we closed. Our system went down, and I didn't access her file until then. It doesn't explain why she hightailed it out of there."

"Is there a chance you'd like to do more than bump into her?"

"Yeah, I'm interested."

"Addie's special. She's mine and Angela's dearest friend," Andrew said, giving him the least subtle warning.

"Hey, Gray," Angela chimed in.

"Hi, Ang."

Angela and Andrew shared another look. "What if there's a way to make it up to her while getting the chance to talk?"

"I'm listening...."

CHAPTER EIGHT

Gray

Grayson mulled over his late-night conversation with Andrew for the rest of the weekend. Even Minnie didn't distract him with her antics. Factor in his restless night's sleep, and the triple shot he'd added to his latte meant Monday's paperwork was the last thing he wanted to deal with.

Which is why he didn't. Purple hair, pouty lips, and blue eyes filled his screen.

"Why are you staring at Addison Carter's picture?" Jasper asked, giving him a knowing smirk, striding into Gray's office unannounced.

"Why are you here on your day off?" Gray countered, clicking out of Addison's profile.

"Says the guy who sees me every Monday."

"Still doesn't change the fact that you can stay home, snuggle someone while edging someone until they scream."

Jasper grunted. "You know it's not in the cards for me. I captured love once, and she slipped away."

Gray knew some of what happened between Jess and Jasper, though not the entire story. He didn't know if anyone did. "You can go after her, you know?"

Jasper's voice grew distant when he said, "I can't. My wife needs to come to me."

Well, that was a loaded answer if Gray ever heard one.

Gray leaned back in his chair and pinned his friend with a look. "While you wait, are you gonna keep working your matchmaking magic on everyone around you?" he asked, folding his arms across his chest and waiting Jasper out.

Gray didn't have to wait long.

"It worked then?"

Ever seen a bear of a man look downright gleeful? It's kind of fucking scary.

"Tell me how she liked the club and you."

Gray sighed and dropped his defensive stance. "I kind of fucked it up."

"Please tell me you didn't do something stupid to hurt or insult her," Jasper growled.

Okay, now it's Gray's turn to be pissed.

"Hold up. Since when in all the years you've known me have I ever hurt or insulted a woman?"

Jasper raised his hands in surrender. "Matty...," he said, softening his voice and using the nickname they'd given him when he joined his unit. "I apologize."

"It's okay." He sighed, more irritated with himself than with his friend.

"What I meant is, Addison has gone through a lot, and I hope you didn't rebuff her." Jasper shrugged. "She's Andrew's oldest and dearest friend. I like her and want the best for her. I believe it's you. Tell me I'm wrong."

Gray stilled and met Jasper's penetrating gaze, answering him, "You're not. I wanted her from the moment I spied her waterfall of purple hair."

"Then I don't get it. How did you fuck things up?"

"The monitoring session ran longer than expected, and I didn't get to the lobby in time to meet her, so Kari allowed her inside to explore on her own."

"I'll speak to Kari and remind her to follow the instructions attached to someone's file when she checks it."

"Already talked to her, and it's my fault for the vague note. I didn't know about the issues with the server because your micromanaging ass took care of it."

Jasper winced. "Shit, sorry, man. I figured you'd be busy with Addison by then. I didn't know you missed her."

"Well, I found her in front of the main stage, lost in a scene. I didn't realize until after that the woman and Addison were the same person. She, uh, I don't know…."

"She drew you in?"

"Like a moth to a flame, brother. The next thing I knew, she walked right into me, and I didn't want to let her go. All those luscious curves, gorgeous purple hair, and sweet vanilla scent. Fuck, she's something else."

Gray ran his hand through his hair, frustrated because of what happened next. "Then she beat feet out of the club. Ran out the door like I'd chase after her. Maybe she wanted me to chase after her. Fuck, I almost did."

Gray leaned forward in his chair. "By the way, we need a better software system. We can't go without access to guest profiles."

"Already looking into it. I'll have some options for us to review in the next few days. This won't happen again."

"I figured you'd already be on it."

Jasper nodded, then asked, "What will you do about Addison besides moon over her picture?"

"Well, there's a plot twist of others working behind the scenes to assist your matchmaking efforts," he alluded, enjoying Jasper's eagerness to know who. The man sure did love, love. It's too bad things didn't work out for him and Jess. Gray hoped he'd give someone a chance again someday.

"Don't leave me in suspense."

"Andrew called me Saturday night after he and Angela met Addie for dinner. When she left the club, she came home to a burst pipe in her apartment and a middle-of-the-night move to a hotel."

"This all happened on her birthday?"

"Yup."

"Damn. The poor girl. Is there anything we can do?"

"Andrew mentioned there's something I can do."

Jasper nodded, acknowledging his singular vernacular. If anyone's helping Addison Carter, it'll be Gray.

"Addison is looking to buy a place out my way, and Andrew asked me to help."

"And you've talked?"

"Not yet, no."

Jasper got up from the chair across from him. "How about you do that by the end of the day? Ask her to meet you at the cute coffee shop near the station. Give her your agent's name and show her the sights. Use the opportunity to get to know her, and perhaps you can convince her to give your sorry ass a chance."

Then Jasper threw him one more piece of advice on his way out. "Don't fuck this up, Matty. And if you make plans for tomorrow, take the night off. You covered for me on Friday. Consider it payback. It's not like I won't be here, anyway."

When his door closed, and Gray was alone, he opened a new email. It's time to charm the elusive Addison Carter into meeting for coffee.

CHAPTER NINE

Addie

Monday.

Three days after 'floodgate,' Addie is over this hotel life. Little sleep and a slight hangover kind of weekend meant this particular Monday hit rougher than most.

Addie had five hundred words left before she hit her daily word count, and then she needed to return to the apartment and put the rest of her belongings into storage. Harold, the super, informed her they'd removed the excess water, and fans almost had things dried out.

She searched for the motivation to get up and get dressed when an email notification from Club Decadent got her attention. She opened the message to find it was not from Jasper.

The sex god sent her an email.

From: Grayson Matthews

To: Addison Carter

Subject: Sorry about Friday night

Hi Addison.

I apologize for not being in the lobby to meet you and escort you inside. I'd like to have the chance to make it up to you. Whenever you want to come to the club again, let me know, and I'd be happy to give you a tour and answer your questions.

On another subject, our mutual friend believes I can help point you in the right direction with a real estate agent in New Haven. I'm sure the agent I used can help you find the perfect property.

I know it's a bit of a jaunt, but will you have coffee with me tomorrow? You familiarize yourself with the area, or at least make sure you're okay with the lengthy commute when you need to make it.

Anyway, let me know.

I look forward to making things up to you, Addison.

Talk soon,

Gray

"Well, isn't Andrew full of all kinds of surprises? He and I are going to chat... later." Grayson is asking her out for coffee.

Don't ignore the zing.

Addie hoped her response didn't appear too eager.

From: Addison Carter

To: Grayson Matthews

Subject: Re: Sorry about Friday night

Hello Grayson.

Yes, to both. Here's my number: 212-555-5309. Text me the address, and we can discuss the rest tomorrow in person.

Chat soon,

Addie

Is it too direct? Or too flirty? Addie wanted to say, 'Call me.' She knew if she heard his sexy-as-sin voice in her ear, her panties would catch on fire. Thirty seconds later, her phone buzzed.

Hmm...who is the eager one here?

> **Unknown Number: Hi**

Unknown Number: The address is 5566 Main Street. It's a 5 to 10-minute walk from the station.

Unknown Number: Now you have my number <smiley face emoji>

Addie smiled and added him to her contacts.

Addison: Hi. Is 2pm OK?

Addison: It'll give me time to work in the morning, then head there.

Grayson: Works for me. Want me to pick you up?

Addison: Thanks for the offer. I want to walk and check out the area.

Addison: See you at 2.

Grayson: Can't wait.

love

Addie fell in love with New Haven the moment she stepped off the train. Knowing she'd have this kind of tranquility while still being able to access the city's vibrancy filled her with excitement and possibilities.

The bell above the door jingled when Addie entered the café where she and Grayson had agreed to meet. She searched the occupied tables, not finding anyone who fit the description of a *leather-clad sex-god* waiting for someone.

Addie approached the counter to grab a coffee and something sweet. Once she got her dose of caffeine and something to soothe her sweet tooth, she'd snag a table.

One of the two college-age girls behind the counter stepped forward. "Hi there. What can I get for you?"

"Hi. Can I get a medium dark roast with vanilla oat milk and one of those amazing-looking chocolate-filled croissants?"

The brunette gave her a smile and said, "Sure thing. Is that everything, Ma'am?"

Addie winced. "Yes."

"$7.35, please."

"Thanks." Addie gave her a ten-spot and told her to keep the change.

"Here you go, Ma'am. Enjoy."

A second, Ma'am? All right, the point's made, Miss Young *and attractive twenty-year-old. Fun fact: twenty turns into forty* awfully quickly.

Addie didn't say those things aloud. She didn't want to traumatize a super polite person and retrieved her food without further comment.

Choosing a table in the corner, Addie nibbled on the croissant and sipped her coffee, she scrolled through the local listings she found online and worried about finding something in her price range.

Distracted by her research, it took a second to register the sound of the bell above the door, signaling someone else had entered the shop.

Addie lifted her eyes, and her gaze collided with the dark eyes she almost convinced herself she imagined. She smiled and gave Grayson a wave, which turned into a weird claw-like hand gesture.

WTF? Ugh, Addie, don't be lame on your date.

Nope...not a date. Zing or no zing, he's way too young and out of your league. Wait. Why is he out of her league? She's forty and fine. Why can't she have some fun?

Grayson headed her way instead of going to the counter to place his order. "Hi, Addison. It's nice to meet you." He held his hand out for her to take. "I'm Grayson Matthews. Please call me Gray."

His voice, oh man, his voice. If melted chocolate has a sound...if her first cup of coffee in the morning has a sound...his voice embodies such a deep, smooth sound.

"Please call me Addie," she said, sounding soft and breathy when his palm enveloped hers.

Zing. Zing. Zing.

Shit. Shit. Shit.

"I hope you don't mind if I leave my cell on vibrate," she said, extracting her hand from his. "There's a call I'm expecting about a temporary apartment. I need a better option than the hotel I'm staying at."

"Of course. Happy birthday, by the way. Andrew told me about the burst pipe. I'm also sorry about what happened at the club."

"You already apologized, and thank you," Addie said, unable to stop her smile.

"Can I get you a refill?" he asked.

"I'm fine, thanks."

His gaze shifted to her half-eaten treat, then back to her with interest. "Looks yummy."

"It's delicious."

"Hmm." Gray leaned forward and swiped his thumb against the corner of her lip. The contact made her skin tingle. When he showed her the flaky crumb and dab of chocolate on his thumb and then sucked it into his mouth, she gasped.

"You're right. It is delicious. Thanks for helping me decide what I want. I'll be right back."

Her mouth dropped open, and her eyes stayed on the most gorgeous ass she'd ever seen when Gray made his way to the counter.

"Okay," Addie mumbled, too stunned to say anything else.

Did she greet the hottest man she'd ever met with food on her face? Is her underwear damp with arousal because of the way Grayson dealt with it?

*Yeah…*yeah, *she did.*

High-pitched giggles reached her ears.

Addie looked up to find Grayson attempting to place his order during an overzealous attempt at flirting from the girls behind the counter.

She tried to keep her spying discreet, viewing the exchange from beneath her lashes. Addie smiled to herself when Gray extricated himself with polite precision and headed back to their table.

Gray turned and graced her with a gorgeous smile.

"Happen often?" Addie asked when he set his coffee and croissant down on the table. To answer, he pulled his chair beside hers and sat close enough for her to feel the warmth radiating from him.

"Sometimes. Though I let all the aggressive flirters know I'm a big scary Dom with many devices to tie them up to torture orgasms out of them all night long."

How did Addie become the person tied up in this scenario?

Gray laughed. "Oh, man. The look on your face. I'm kidding, I swear." He leaned closer, wanting to share a secret. "Truth. I tell only the people I'm interested in doing those things, too."

Holy hot damn, Batman.

Flabbergasted, Addie asked, "Are you flirting with me?"

"Um, I'm trying? Since you're calling me out, I'm doing a terrible job." His deep chuckle rumbled between them. "Let me try this again."

Gray leaned closer, and electricity sparked between them, reminding Addie of the instant chemistry she witnessed with Angela and Andrew.

Addie found it more and more challenging to keep a polite distance.

This is crazy, right?

"It's not the quality I'm questioning. It's why?"

"I don't understand."

Did she need to spell it out?

"No. I don't understand why you...." Yes, she waved her hands in front of his face, encompassing everything from his waist up in a circular motion.

Addie concluded that the more interested she was in someone, the more awkward she became.

"You, a stunning specimen of male yumminess who's at least ten years younger than me, can land a woman half my age... I have to ask. Why the interest in me?"

As if Addie had pushed him, Gray fell back against his chair.

"I-"

Gray held up his hand, stopping the further insertion of her foot into her mouth.

"I may need a second. That's a lot to absorb."

"Okay."

She guessed Grayson meant second in the literal sense when he grabbed the arm of her chair, turned her toward him, and pulled her close until her knees tucked between his thick, muscular thighs.

With his hands still gripping the arms of her chair, Gray leaned into her personal space and said, "First, thank you for the compliment. I don't recall being called a 'stunning specimen of male yumminess' ever. Second." Grayson removed a folded paper from the pocket of his leather jacket. He unfolded it and handed it to her. She recognized it right away.

Oh, shit.

Addie swallowed, trying to clear her throat. "Um, where'd you get this?"

"An employee found it at the club by her counter. She brought it to my attention, believing I'd find it interesting."

Addie fidgeted in her seat. "I can understand why you might."

Where's the spontaneous giant pit ready to swallow her when a girl needed it?

"For the record, I didn't spy on you or anything nefarious. I wrote this description weeks ago while plotting out my latest novel. I'm a romance author, or at least trying to be."

Addie blew out an exasperated breath. "I didn't know a character I envisioned could have a real-life doppelgänger. I've never seen you before Friday night, I swear."

"Oh, you mean when you buried your face in my chest and gave me a lungful of the sweetest vanilla scent I've ever smelled?"

He loves the way she smells? Why is that so hot?

"Kari googled you and found your book. Pretty sure that means you are definitely an author."

"Oh, my God. Please tell me you didn't read it." Addie did not want this man reading her student/teacher erotic fuckfest.

"Swear I didn't. Though Kari did something... she said she one-clicked it?"

"I can never return to the club again," Addie muttered. Then her head shot up, and she looked Gray dead in the eye. "Never ask her about it; if she tries to tell you anything, put your fingers in your ears and sing the *Lalalas*. Promise me."

"Okay. Okay, I promise," Gray said, holding up his hands in surrender.

"Look, I understand that may seem like an extreme reaction from someone who wants to make a living selling her books, but it's different when strangers buy them."

"It's not a bad first release... and please tell Kari thanks for purchasing it. I appreciate it, but... I have this thing about someone I know telling me they've read my book, and I haven't gotten comfortable with it happening yet."

"It's all good." Gray smiled, and mischief sparkled in his dark eyes. "Can I say you may have manifested me into your life?"

"I- yes...?"

Hmm, manifestation... is one way to describe it.

"Addie," he groaned, and she loved how it made her name sound. "This," Gray did a much less intense version of her encompassing hand gesture, "is real. This attraction is real, and I want to pursue whatever is happening here."

Gray's face dipped closer to hers. "I also want to help provide some of the hands-on inspiration you seek."

Addie stopped herself from uttering, *Oh... oh, fuck.* And went with a more subtle, "Oh, okay."

"As for the age thing. Did you misrepresent yours on the driver's license you provided?"

"What? No." Did he read everything else she provided? Like the extensive kinky questionnaire? Addie bit down on her lower lip, hard.

"To answer the unasked question written all over your beautiful face. Yes, I read everything you provided." Gray's heated look implied he remembered every word, too.

"Has anyone else?"

"Jasper did. He reads and vets every client's application. Since your date of birth's accurate, you'll have to cut our age gap in half, Addie."

"You're thirty-five?"

Grayson chuckled. "Yup. Closer to thirty-six now. Birthdays in mid-February, in case you wanted to mark your calendar," he added with a wink.

"Ha-ha." Addie clasped her hands a little tighter in her lap in case they got some bright ideas of their own and did something crazy like reach for her phone to make a note of it.

Valentine's baby?

"The fifteenth, to be specific." He relayed like an expert mind reader. "A four-and-a-half-year age gap doesn't sound bad, does it?"

"Um, no...."

Addie studied him from beneath her eyelashes. Outside the club, Grayson's style is sexy casual with his fitted t-shirt, dark denim, leather boots, and jacket. Heck, the girls behind the counter bent over it, trying to get his attention.

Yet Gray remained focused on her, offering his hand for her to take. Addie slid her fingers across his palm, linking them together.

"What are you proposing?"

Gray laughed at her choice of words. "Let's keep it simple for now. I want to get to know you and give you pleasure and romance. After reading your club questionnaire, it turns out we have a lot in common, and we'd have a fuckton of fun exploring this."

He leaned even closer. "Let me take you out, Addie. I have a place in the city I use when working. You can come back to the club, and I'll give you the tour you missed out on, answer your questions, and if there's anything you'd like to try, we can discuss it. All options are on the table."

CHAPTER TEN

Gray

Addie's lips parted, her answer on the tip of her tongue, when her cell vibrated on the table between them. "It's the rental office," she said, reaching for her phone.

"I hope it's good news."

Addie gave him a dazzling smile. "Me too." Then she stepped away from the table and answered, "Hello?"

Gray tried to curb his asshole-ness when he realized a big part of him didn't want her to get it.

He wanted her to stay with him.

From the moment he walked in and saw her, his heart stuttered. Gray wanted more.

The bell jingled above him, and the smell of fresh coffee and baked treats made his mouth water. The hint of vanilla made him search for Addison, finding her at a table in the corner.

She stared at her phone, and Gray stared at her, catching the furrow of worry between her brows. And he wanted to be the one to take those worries away.

Addison glanced up, sensing his presence, and he received the full effect of her beautiful blue eyes in the light of day.

His heart stuttered when their gazes met. Warmth filled his chest beneath his Carpe diem tattoo.

Seize the day indeed....

Gray didn't mean to eavesdrop. Addie didn't go far, making it easy to hear her side. "Yes, this is Addison. Yes, the one-bedroom. I see...okay, I understand. If something else comes up in the next couple of weeks...yes, okay. Thank you, goodbye."

He winced when Addie dropped her phone back on the table. "What happened?" he asked, though he'd already guessed.

"Oh, a film company offered the rental company double the posted rent to scoop up every unit they have available for the next eight weeks."

"Oh, Addie, I'm sorry." And Gray was, despite his earlier thoughts to the contrary. "What are the odds they'll have something else?"

"Almost nonexistent," she finished. "I'm not sure what I'll do except keep looking."

Addie slumped in her chair. "Ugh, I'm already crawling up the walls of my hotel room, and the bill will max out my credit card. It is what it is, I guess. Money isn't the issue. I'd just rather put those funds toward purchasing a home."

"Move in with me," Gray blurted.

Shit. Not cool.

"What?" Addie's eyes widened, and she opened and closed her mouth several times, not knowing what to say.

He'd shot his shot in the worst way. Gray saw the word 'no' forming on her lips, and he didn't blame her. "Hear me out. You want to purchase something in the area, right?"

"Yes."

"And you also need a temporary place to stay for the next while, one with a comfortable writing space?"

"Yes, but...."

Gray pressed on, stopping Addie from finishing that thought. "My house has four bedrooms on the second floor, all with an ensuite, and the primary suite I use is on the ground floor. You can have the entire upstairs to yourself. There's an office with a beautiful view you can use to write, and besides sharing the kitchen, it'd be like having your own place."

The adorable furrow between Addie's brows returned while she considered his offer.

"You can look for property around here worry-free and make the trip into the city when you want or need to while having a safe place to stay and, if I say so myself, a beautiful place to write."

"I-We don't know each other. This is crazy, right? I can't impose on you. What if I cramp your style?"

Gray kept his expression neutral, while inside, he cheered. Addie didn't say no.

"You won't cramp my style, Addie. In fact, you'll be the first person to stay in my house since I finished the renovations. If you agree to stay." Gray reached over and rubbed her knuckles with his thumb. The slow back and forth soothed them both.

"If you want to keep things platonic, we can. I'm in the city three days a week for work, so you'll have the place to yourself. You'll do me a favor by looking after things when I'm not there. It's a win-win for both of us."

Addie pulled her hand away and crossed her arms in a protective gesture. "You're not a kidnapping murderer, are you?"

Gray laughed. "I swear. Not a kidnapper or murderer."

"Well, I'd insist on paying my share of expenses."

"I don't need the money. How about you save it for the place you plan to buy?"

"I don't know...."

"No pressure. I wanted you to know the option is there if you want it."

Gray let the subject rest and was about to ask Addie if she wanted another coffee when she surprised him by asking, "What about the rest?"

"The rest?" Gray needed her to be specific.

"You know...the getting to know me, and the help with my, um...research. The, uh, fucking you mentioned wanting to do...which I'd also like to do." Addie's cheeks heated with a blush.

Gray leaned in, bringing his lips close to her ear. "Those options are all on the table if you want them." Then he leaned back, meeting her curious gaze. "There's no pressure to do anything beyond talk. You can ask me whatever you like, and I'll always be forthright with you."

"Okay."

He needed a bit more. "Okay?"

"Yes, I'll take you up on using your second floor."

Gray wanted to shout for joy but remained seated at the table.

"This is temporary. I'm calling your agent when I return to the city, and you'll have your place back to yourself again. Let's play the rest by ear and ensure we like each other."

Gray chuckled. "I'm pretty sure we like each other, Addie." He enjoyed her blush deepening with his declaration. "One more thing. Do you have allergies?"

"Like dust or pollen? No."

"How about cats?"

CHAPTER ELEVEN

Addie

*D*id she agree to move in with someone she's met twice?

On the return trip to the city, Addie made the best of her window seat and opened her group chat with Andrew and Angela. She needed her friend's support and reassurance that she wasn't out of her damn mind for doing this.

> **Addie: I'm staying with Grayson while I look for a place to buy.**

> **Addie: You know...in case he's a serial killer <skull and crossbones emoji>**

> **Addie: I need you to tell me I'm doing the right thing.**

> **Addie: Please**

Angela: ...

Andrew: ...

Angela: WHAT?? He's not a serial killer. I will, however, give a RIP to your <cat with wry smile emoji> cause she's going to be wrecked for anyone else. LOL.

Okay, not a serial killer. Good to know. Perhaps a destroyer of pussies? Also, a good thing to know.

Andrew: He's a good man, Addie. Don't let the speed at which you're going scare you. Gray isn't the type to disobey your boundaries. He will push your limits in ways you've always deserved.

Andrew: ...

Andrew: It also seems my Angel needs to be disciplined when this conversation ends. Be ready, darling wife.

Addie knew the saucy comment would place her friend in a compromising position. She also suspected it was her intention.

Angela: Always ready, darling husband

Addie: <face vomiting emoji> <rolling on the floor laughing emoji>

Addie: Srsly tho thx 4 the support, u guys

Andrew: Stop texting like a teenager. We're elder millennials. We type shit out.

Addie: <winking face with tongue emoji>

Andrew: And you're welcome. Remember to enjoy the ride. <winking face emoji>

Addie: I will

Angela: <eggplant emoji> <peach emoji>

Andrew: Angel...

Addie smiled and put her phone away, looking forward to whatever came next.

Gray showed up at her hotel room at the crack of dawn with coffee and breakfast wraps, insisting she eat while he got her stuff to his vehicle.

He grabbed the last box on the third trip, and Addie picked up the last bag. She checked the bathroom, closet, and under the bed, ensuring she left nothing behind.

"Ready?" Gray asked with a chuckle while she did one last deep dive under the bed.

"Yup," Addie confirmed, popping up from the floor. She completed her checkout online and can leave without further delay. "Let's go meet your cat."

They took the I-95 north; the scenery changing from skyscrapers and villages to green fields until they eventually pulled onto a gravel drive.

"We're here," Grayson said, pulling Addie's gaze to the house at the top of the drive. "Welcome to Stone Barn Farm."

"Oh, wow."

Gray lived in a white two-story farmhouse with a wraparound porch framed with flowers and greenery.

"It's named after what's now my workshop," he said, pointing to the barn with stone walls. He brought his SUV to a stop by the porch steps and shut off the engine, letting Addie take it all in.

His nearest neighbors aren't even visible.

"It's beautiful." Addie opened the passenger door and took in a deep, cleansing breath. Maybe not on as grand a scale, but she wanted to find a place like this.

"Wait until you get a look at the inside. Come on, I'll bring your stuff in a minute. Let me show you around, and you can pick which room you want."

"Okay." Sharing his excitement, Addie took his offered hand, and Gray linked their fingers together, tugging her up the porch steps.

When they reached the landing, Addie turned to take it all in. "When surrounded by concrete, it's hard to wrap your mind around this being a train ride away." Addie wanted to move closer when Gray leaned against the railing beside her.

"I get it." Gray rolled the sleeves of his shirt up, and those muscular, tattooed forearms sprinkled with dark hair drew Addie's attention like a moth to a flame.

Gray kept talking, oblivious to her new and very specific forearm kink. "Every time I come home, the absolute silence amazes me."

"Oh, I'll need a vehicle if I buy a place here. I-I haven't driven in ages. I'm not sure I remember how. Is it like riding a bike? I won't forget, right?" Addie did a piss-poor job of hiding the panic in her voice.

Gray cupped her shoulder and ran his hand up and down her arm. "Listen, I use the Escalade maybe once a week. It's yours to borrow while you're here, and if you need a driving refresher, I'll give you lessons."

His voice dropped, and Addie wanted to believe Gray meant more than driving lessons.

She blushed at the very idea. "You've done so much already. I can't use your vehicle too, Gray."

"Fuuuck," he groaned, and his grip tightened with possessiveness. "Say it again," Gray demanded, while his intense gaze ensnared hers.

"What?" She wracked her brain for what she'd said to garner such a reaction. Did he mean his name? "Gray?"

"Mm-hm." Gray's other hand went to her waist, and he tugged her closer, dipping his head toward hers. His hand moved from her shoulder to her face. His palm heated her skin while his thumb skated over her cheekbone. "Addie." His breath whispered across her lips when he said her name, making her shudder.

Gray nudged her nose with his. The man took anticipation to another level, letting his breath ghost across her lips again.

"Please kiss me, Gray." His lips touched hers, passion sparking between them, and —

A loud "Mrrrrrraaaaooooowww" sounded inside the house, followed by a claw-tipped paw sliding down a glass pane.

Addie opened her eyes and peered over Gray's shoulder into a set of narrowed golden ones. An enormous white and black patchwork cat stared back at her.

"Oh, shit." Addie jumped out of his grasp. She swore the oversized feline was giving her the stink-eye.

Gray rubbed his hand over his face and groaned, "Damn cock-blocking cat." He gave Addie a rueful smile and reached for her hand. "Come on, let me introduce you to Minnie."

Gray unlocked the door, swinging it wide, and a moment later, the furball barreled toward them, jumping into his waiting arms like he expected the tackle.

"Oh, my God," Addie muttered.

The beast purred, rubbing against Gray, eager to mark its territory. "This is Minnie?" Addie asked. She must weigh at least forty pounds. "Did you name her in an Alanis Morrisette *Ironic* sort of way?"

Gray chuckled and scratched Minnie under her chin. The purring increased in volume. "Swear I didn't. I found her in the long grass behind the barn when she was a few weeks old. I looked for her mom, and when I didn't find her, I raised her myself."

"She fit in my hand, and Minnie seemed to suit. I didn't know at the time she was a Maine Coon, or how big she'd grow."

"You rescued her?" A chorus of angelic awes sounded in her head.

"Well, yeah. I Googled what to do, went to the pet store, got some kitten formula, a bottle, toys, a bed, and everything a two-week-old needs." Gray chuckled. "We bonded, and Minnie filled the emotional void the manual labor of renovating this place didn't provide."

"Aw, I'm glad she found you then. I didn't take you for a cat person when I first ran into you."

"You're telling me when your nose landed against my collarbone, the first question to come to mind was, is this guy a cat person?"

Addie's face went up in flames. "Well, shit. I held the door open and walked right into that one. Didn't I?"

Gray's deep laughter warmed her insides. "Yeah, you kind of did."

Addie scratched Minnie beneath her chin, and the cat gave her hand a welcoming head-butt. "She's like a giant poof-ball."

The next second, Minnie jumped from Gray's shoulder and sauntered away with her tail up in a fuck-you kind of gesture. "Huh. Well, then."

"Don't take it to heart. Give Minnie food, a thorough chin scratch, and I swear you'll be BFFs for life."

With the cat getting its due, Addie turned and took everything in. From the classic look outside, she didn't expect the open, modern floor plan in shades of blue, grey, and cream on the inside. High ceilings and vast windows made it bright, warm, and inviting.

"You mentioned doing the renovations yourself? This is amazing work."

"The guys helped with the bigger projects, and I used a designer for specific areas. It's mine, though. I worked on all of it," Gray said with pride.

The kitchen, living, and dining area made up the front part of the house, with a hall leading to the back.

Will the tour include Gray's bedroom?

Addie cleared her throat and redirected her lustful thoughts. "This staircase is beautiful. Is it original to the house?" she asked, unable to resist running her hand over the carved wood.

"Yeah, this area used to be divided into small rooms, and the stairway overpowered the narrow hallway. We demolished the walls and opened it up. The staircase became a functional art piece in the center of it all."

They moved further into the house, getting a better look at what his kitchen offered. It seemed Gray possessed all the bells and whistles. Gas stovetop, large kitchen island, double oven, and a fridge big enough to get lost in. Damn...she hoped he didn't mind her making use of it.

"With a setup like this, I hope you cook."

"Yeah, the other option is to starve, and I like to eat." The way his gaze scorched over her, Addie got the impression he'd like to eat her, and her lady bits got super excited.

Like Gray read her mind, he chuckled and asked, "What about you?"

"Oh, um. Same. Barry, my ex, was a lousy cook. If I didn't do it, we'd live off takeout."

"Oh, sorry. Together a long time?"

"Married almost nineteen years when I walked in on him and our neighbor dirtying my sheets."

Gray's face reddened with anger. "I can't believe someone disrespected you in such a way."

"Yeah, well, he's an ex for a reason. We completed our divorce several months ago."

"Do you have kids?" he asked, then backtracked. "You don't have to answer. It's too personal a question. I apologize."

"No, it's fine. We have a daughter named Sadie. She's in her first year at university." Addie wasn't sure she was ready to hear this answer, though she asked anyway. "Do you have children or want children?"

"No," he answered with no hesitation. "Did I contemplate having kids? Yeah, and I realized it's not something I wanted. For the record, I have no issue dating someone who's a parent. Are more kids something you want?"

Addie sagged with relief. "God, no. The idea of doing it over again gives me hives. I just wanted to know where you stood on the topic."

"Sounds like I'm standing in the same place as you. No desire to have kids. Made the decision permanent with a vasectomy two years ago."

"Cool."

Oh my god, she did not say getting the snip is cool.

"Um, yeah. You did." Gray tried to disguise his laughter with a coughing fit while Addie tried not to die from embarrassment.

"Um...." She bit her lip and ran her fingers over the smooth granite countertop, more than ready to circle back to the subject of cooking. "I love baking. It helps when I have writer's block. Eating it by myself afterward is the problem."

"Well, you're welcome to whatever I've got in the kitchen. I'll go to the grocery store if I don't have what you need."

Gray leaned closer to confide, "I'm partial to brownies or chocolate chip cookies."

Addie breathed in his spicy, masculine scent and almost moaned at how good he smelled. "Cook me dinner occasionally, and you've got yourself a deal. Endless tasty treats any day of the week."

His heated gaze trailed over her, pausing on her lips and her tits before traveling the rest of the way down her body.

"I can agree with those terms."

Much to Addie's disappointment, he didn't touch her and continued with the tour. Gray pointed to two doors on the left, on the other side of the fridge. "Those lead to the pantry and basement, and the single door on the right is a powder room. My bedroom's at the end of the hall."

Gray didn't take her there. He placed a hand at the base of her spine and guided her upstairs. Addie added an extra sway to her hips. Biting her lip, she giggled when Gray groaned behind her and said, "You play dirty, Ms. Carter."

"I don't know what you mean, Mr. Matthews."

Gray cleared his throat, pausing on the landing. "I'm going to bring your things inside. Look around and choose whichever room you want."

He pointed to a door. "The storage room is there, and the office is across from it. I'll be right back." Addie heard the front door close and poked her head into each room.

The first bedroom looked sunny and bright, with a creamy yellow interior. It's nice, but it's a little...Addie laughed. Is she Goldie, and does this place belong to the Three Bears? This room didn't have the right vibe. She moved on to the next one.

Done in shades of grey and white, with large windows overlooking the backyard. Addie loved it and didn't need to look at the other two, but she gave them the briefest of perusals to appease her curiosity. They're beautiful. The one overlooking the backyard remained her favorite.

Addie heard Gray set some of her belongings inside. She'd help him in a minute, wanting to peek at the office space he offered her to use.

Built-in shelves took up one wall while the desk spanned another. There's a view of the barn, a grassy field, and the forest beyond it.

She pictured her days writing here as if it were the most natural thing in the world.

Addie jumped when Gray appeared in the doorway, one of her bags in each hand. "You picked the bedroom overlooking the backyard, didn't you?"

"Yes. How did you know?"

"Just a hunch."

"I can take those," Addie said, reaching for her bags.

Gray kept them out of her reach. "I got it."

"No, it's okay. I can bring the rest of my belongings up. If your leg's bothering you, you don't need to go up and down the stairs a dozen times on my account."

Gray gave her a sharp look, and Addie bit her lip, worried she'd overstepped. "Sorry, I saw you favoring your left leg when you went downstairs and didn't want to cause you unnecessary discomfort."

"I'm fine, I promise. It's an old injury, and my leg gets stiff now and then." Addie sensed he didn't tell her everything and chose not to press the matter.

"Thanks again for letting me stay here."

"Of course. Do you like the space? I finished painting the office last week."

"It's my-I mean, it's a dream workspace." She blushed, catching her slip. "I can't believe you're letting me use it while you have all your stuff crammed in the room across the hall."

Grayson put her bags down and stepped into the room. "I want you to use it while you're here. I can make the other space work."

Gray came a little closer, and Addie held her breath, hoping he might pick up where they left off on the porch. Gray stopped in front of her, turning her to face the windows. The heat of his body warmed her, yet he kept a space between them out of respect or perhaps restraint.

Addie didn't know. She also didn't ask.

"I hope you'll find inspiration here."

"Me too." They grew quiet, standing close, not touching except for his hands on her shoulders. Addie wanted to lean into him.

"Listen, Addie." Gray turned her to face him. "I'll help you bring the rest of your things upstairs, and then I'll let you get settled. I'm taking the train into the city this afternoon to work tonight."

"You are? I never would've made you drive there and back if I'd known you worked tonight."

"You didn't make me," he growled, and desire pooled deep in her belly. "I wanted to. This way, you can settle in, write, and focus on finding the perfect property. Plus, you can bond with Minnie until I return tomorrow afternoon."

"Oh, okay." Addie didn't mean to sound disappointed. She hoped they'd talk about sexual activity-type things...or at least get back to the kiss Minnie interrupted.

Dang it.

"It's my four-day weekend after tonight's shift. We can have dinner and discuss what we want to do while you're here, and then I'll show you around the rest of the place."

"There's more?"

A hint of a sultry smile touched Grayson's full lips. "I left a couple of things off your initial tour. I want to show you after we talk."

The barn? His bedroom? Why did she picture the barn first?

"Okay."

Gray leaned toward her, and Addie braced herself. This is it. He's going to kiss her. Then. To her utter confusion, he squeezed her arm and stepped back.

"Let's bring the rest of your stuff up, okay?"

"Sounds great."

Why didn't he kiss her?

CHAPTER TWELVE

Gray

*D*amn it. Why didn't he kiss Addie?

Gray wanted to. Fuck, he wanted to.

They needed to talk first and define all the depraved things Addie desired and how Gray wanted to help her experience every single one of them.

She's in his house right now, unpacking her belongings, making herself at home, and setting up the office how she wants. When Gray walked in and saw Addie gazing out the window, he knew the space belonged to her.

He'd renovate the storage room and make it a second office. His. Besides, he loved a project.

The club opened in less than two hours, and there are more pressing things to do than sit here daydreaming about Addie. It didn't stop him from doing it anyway. Until a brisk rap on his door preceded Kari waltzing into his office.

Not yet dressed for her shift, she still wore her blue jeans and pink t-shirt, reminding him of how young and sweet she was.

Unless she's up to trouble.

"Oh-my-god, oh-my-god, oh-my-god. Gray, you've got to read this."

Gray braced himself to tackle whatever emergency Kari might have uncovered when she handed him her tablet.

She didn't hand him a work tablet.

...Stacey wore her shortest skirt and left the buttons of her white uniform shirt undone, hoping Professor Beatty saw the red lace peeking between the material.

His gaze zeroed in on her the moment she took her seat. "Ms. Forester, please remain after class. I need to speak with you."

"Yes, Professor." Stacey hoped he'd do more than speak to her since she planned to offer her virginity...

Gray dropped what turned out to be Kari's eReader face down on his desk. "Kari," he growled. "Please tell me this isn't what I think it is."

"Well, if you believe it's anything other than Addison's book, I'd question how many erotic romance authors you know."

"I can't read it."

"Since when have you been a prude?"

"Addie made me promise not to."

She looked at him strangely. "Kind of an odd request from someone who publishes their work with the hopes of it being read."

Hm...Kari's got a point. Is Addie insecure about her writing despite her initial success? It's something he'd have to ask her.

Kari sat on the edge of his desk and asked, "Addie, huh?" She crossed her arms, and Gray knew she was gearing up to interrogate him. "Forget the book. Have you talked to Addison Carter since Friday night?"

Gray wrestled with how much to tell her. Kari's like a little sister, and he wanted to share his excitement. "Addison's at my house right now," he confided, then covered his mouth with his hand, stopping him from spilling more.

Kari smacked his chest. "Shut up."

"Alright, if you don't want to hear anymore." She smacked him two more times for good measure.

"Gray. Do not play with me."

"I'm not. I offered Addie the upper floor of my house because her apartment flooded. She's looking to buy a place out my way, and I want to help her."

"But...?"

"But...?"

"Ugh, getting information from you is like pulling teeth, Gray. There's more, right? You like her?"

"Yeah, I do." No sense in denying it.

"Fuck, I knew it."

"Language," he admonished, though not his place to do so, and she knew it.

Kari rolled her eyes and stood. "Fine, I won't pry for any more details. However, I will make you tell this story on your wedding day."

Married?

Gray coughed and asked, "Can I maybe date her first?"

"Sure. It won't stop your marriage from happening. Just delay it a little. I gotta get ready."

Kari held up her eReader. "You know, while a little cliché with the whole student-professor thing...your woman has a way of writing a low-down dirty sex scene...and the dirty talk? Chef's kiss," she said, kissing her fingertips. "She has a gift."

Kari left, and it's a good thing she did. Otherwise, Gray might snatch her reader back and find out for himself. He didn't. A promise is a promise. Besides, when he got to read Addie's stuff, she'd be the one to read it to him.

Jasper strode in a minute after Kari left with a preoccupied look on his face.

Huh. Is there a sign on the door saying 'Come on in' today?

"I ran into Kari, and she skipped downstairs, refusing to tell me the cause of her excitement. She said to speak with you. Gray, why is our sweet Kari ecstatic, and what does it have to do with you?"

"How about you tell me what's bothering you?" Gray countered.

"Maybe later." Jasper deflected. "How did things go? Are you and Addison the reason for Kari's giddiness?"

"Jasper, I swear you're nosier than a schoolgirl at recess."

"What's your point? You know I'd never betray your confidence. Heck, tell me you're happy, and I'm good."

"I'm happy." However, Gray gave Jasper a little more. "We did the coffee date yesterday, like you suggested. Covered a lot of subjects, including the 'I like you. You like me. Let's see where this goes' conversation."

Gray's devil-may-care confidence wavered, and he didn't quite meet Jasper's eyes when he revealed, "And right now, she's unpacking her things at my house."

Jasper dropped into the chair on the other side of his desk. "Matty...I know you live with a seize-the-day mentality, and for a damn good reason. This is fast, even for you, brother."

"You're right. I live my life to the fullest, grabbing an opportunity when it presents itself because we know better than most; there might not be another chance."

"There are extenuating circumstances. The temporary rental Addie lined up fell through, and I didn't want her to waste her money on an extended hotel stay. So I offered her the second floor of my house. It'll make it easier for her to shop for a property there."

"The logic is sound, and it's quite generous of you. What about the rest? Did you talk about the lifestyle, your specific kinks, the -"

"We touched on a few things, no serious negotiations or anything. I want Addie to get settled and for us to get to know each other. She and I will talk when I get home tomorrow."

"Be right back." Jasper left his office, and Gray heard the beep when he entered his. A minute later, he returned, tossing a small stack of papers on his desk. "There's a blank contract, her paperwork, and a permanent membership courtesy of me."

"Jas..."

He waved his hand. "Addison ended up having a shitty birthday. Tell her it's a gift from us."

A rumbling growl traveled from the pit of his stomach. Gray didn't even realize he'd made it until Jasper's laughter registered. "Or tell her it's from you. Either way, it's good."

"Thanks," he grumbled.

"Why don't you take extra time besides the next few days? Get to know each other. If you're serious and going full speed ahead, take the time to give what you may have a fighting chance."

"You want me to take a vacation? Now?" Gray asked, mulling over the idea of more quality time with Addie.

"I'm here every day. The staff is a well-running unit, and I may need you to take over things while I take some time off soon."

The troubled look on Jasper's face made another appearance. Gray blinked, and it disappeared.

"What did she think when you gave her a tour of your house?"

"I did an amazing job with the renovations."

"Did this tour include the rooms Martha designed?" Jasper asked with a quirked brow.

Gray cleared his throat. "I wanted to save those for after we talked." And he's already second-guessing his decision to do so.

Jasper didn't hide his smirk. He steepled his fingers beneath his chin and said, "Yet you left a curious, erotic romance author alone in your house with a basement sex room and a primary suite kitted out like it graced the pages of Architectural Digest - the sexy boudoir issue?"

Gray's regret over his decision to wait grew by the minute. "The sex room's locked, and the bedroom isn't extravagant."

"It's a Martha design, and screams millions of orgasms await you inside these chamber walls," Jasper said with a laugh.

"Oh, fuck off."

"All I'm saying is she may have some questions when you get home tomorrow." With those parting words, Jasper left Gray's office.

Shit. Gray didn't want to admit Jasper's right. Addie's curiosity will ensure she explores the rest of his house. He almost kicked himself for not being there for her reaction.

Gray's phone lit up with a notification. The sensor above the door to his playroom went off. Seconds later, it went off again. He opened the app and saw the two photos the camera had taken. The top of Addie's head is in the first, and her turned-up face is in the second.

Looks like she found the playroom.

Gray studied the second photo of her upturned face. Fuck, she's beautiful and sexy. He wanted her tied up in his dungeon or draped across his California king, unable to decide which to do first.

Hmm…if she agreed to be, Addie would be the first submissive in his kitted-out sex room. Gray finished the room a few months ago with Martha's design expertise. However, being single and not wanting to bring a rando to his home meant no one else had seen it.

Now he's got a naughty, curious woman to deal with. Gray opened their text thread and sent Addie a message.

CHAPTER THIRTEEN

Addie

A ddie took a box into the bathroom and unpacked her makeup, hair, and moisturizing essentials, filling the empty drawers and shelves with her things. After Gray left, she spent several hours unpacking, saving the office for last.

"Temporary office lent to you by the sexy, sincere, drop-dead gorgeous man also letting you stay in his house." Addie sighed. "Houston, I may have an out-of-control problem of talking to myself."

"Mrrrrrraaaaooooowww." Minnie wound around her legs, eliciting a loud rumbling purr, and Addie gave her a scratch behind her ears.

"Oh, good. I am talking to someone. You'll keep my secrets, won't you, Minnie?" She grunted, hefting the cat into her arms. "Damn, Minnie is the most ironic name ever." And now Alanis' song is stuck in her head.

Addie met the feline's golden gaze. "How about we work on you and I being a team? Addie and Gray for the win?"

Minnie bumped Addie's chin with her head, rubbing against her cheek. "Your opinion means a lot to him."

The cat squirmed free of her arms, done with their conversation, and sauntered off to another part of the house. Addie weighed her options for wooing the finicky feline. "Let's chat again soon," she called after her.

Addie looked around the office, pondering the space. She'd brought her writing essentials, laptop, printer, a color-coded bin of highlighters, a variety of cutesy and inspirational nick-knacks, her mood board... okay, she'd brought all of it.

"I need to contact the real estate agent. No need to get wishful ideas about what it'd be like to stay."

After a shower, Addie clipped her hair into a messy topknot and threw on a pair of comfy sweats and a hoodie. With her phone tucked in the front pocket, she headed to the gorgeous, well-stocked kitchen.

Humming to herself, Addie saw the Echo sitting on the counter. "Alexa? Play Brandi Carlile."

"Playing songs by Brandi Carlile."

She opened the fridge, looking for something to strike her fancy. "Gray didn't lie. He has a bit of everything." She grabbed several ingredients to make a mini charcuterie plate. Slicing some deli meat and cheeses to add beside the grapes, she rinsed.

"Crackers...I need crackers." She pulled open a few cabinets, finding more dishes and gadgets. No biscuits.

"Oh, my God." Addison clutched her chest and jumped when a loud thump sounded behind her. She turned and found Minnie on the counter, stalking her plate full of delicious meats and cheeses.

"Oh no, you don't."

Addie swooped the beast up and deposited her on the floor. She crossed her arms and faced her possible nemesis, who stared up at her with determination. "I doubt your...dad? Owner? Master? Shit, nope, not going there."

Addie squatted, getting eye-level with the cat, hoping she'd listen. "Look, Minnie, I'm sure Gray never lets you walk around on the counters. So, are you testing me, or is this the behavior you display when he's not here?"

"Mrrrrrraaaaoooowww."

"What? You know I don't speak Spanish." Addie snorted. Now she's having a conversation with a cat and quoting Anchorman. Minnie weaved between her legs and then scratched a door off the kitchen.

"Right. The pantry. Hope I can find the crackers and something cat-appropriate for you to eat."

Addie pushed open the door, and the lights turned on. "Is it downstairs?" Minnie meowed and sauntered past her. "I guess it is," she mumbled, letting the cat lead.

When she reached the bottom, Minnie disappeared, and Addie stood in a massive home gym, taking up half the basement's square footage. "Wow. Good to know this is here." Addie enjoyed working out to help get her creative juices flowing.

A door at the back led to a spacious bathroom and mudroom with a door leading outside, not the pantry.

"Minnie? Where are you? You're in big trouble if you double-crossed me and lured me down here to pull a sneak attack and eat my dinner." Addie meant to go back upstairs when another door caught her attention.

The recessed light above the door bathed her in a warm glow when she stood beneath it, shutting off the moment she stepped back, then turning on again when she moved back toward the door.

Addie twisted the handle, and it didn't budge. Locked. Oh, her curiosity's piqued. "What the hell's on the other side of this door?" Her phone buzzed in her pocket, making her jump again.

Since when did she become a nervous nelly?

Gray: Everything OK

"Is he spying on me?" Her gaze darted around the room, looking for hidden cameras. "Geez, Addie. If they're hidden, how will you spot them?"

Despite her friend's reassurances, is Grayson Matthews full of sketchy secrets? At least Drew and Angela will know where to search for her body.

"I need to stop listening to murder and crime podcasts."

Gray: Addie?

"Shit." Almost dropping it, Addie fumbled with her phone, sending a response.

Addie: Everything's great. Found the gym. Is it OK if I use it?

Gray: You're welcome to make use of anything and everything

"Does anything include you? Delete, delete, delete."

Addie: So, you're checking on me?

Gray: ...

Addie eyeballed those typing dots while Gray took his sweet time answering her.

Gray: Not quite

Gray: The door you tried has a sensor attached to an app on my phone

Gulp.

Gray: I'm in my office and saw the notification

Addie: Oh, sorry.

Addie: I didn't mean to snoop; I wanted some crackers, and Minnie lured me into the basement.

Addie: It'll teach me to take directions from a cat

Gray: Minnie will take you where Minnie wants to go

Speaking of the she-devil, Minnie scooted past her up the stairs. "Don't you dare jump on the counter," she yelled, chasing after her.

Addie reached the kitchen in time to catch Minnie mid-jump, much like catching a medicine ball mid-air yet squirmier.

"Mine," Addie informed Minnie when she dropped the cat onto the floor and snatched the plate off the counter.

Addie: No kidding... So...the sensor. Is it for the basement or the room?

Gray: The room

Addison rolled her eyes. "Evasive much."

Addie: Why?

Gray: It's my sex room.

"Oh, shit." This time, she almost dropped her phone and her food.

Well, Addie wanted full disclosure, and she got it.

It's not like it's a surprise. Gray owns and works at a BDSM club. She expected one of those bedrooms upstairs to be decked in leather and chains. To have found them all elegant and ordinary turned into a bit of a letdown.

> **Gray: I planned to show you after we talked.**

> **Gray: If it's something you wanted.**

> **Gray: Otherwise, the room will remain locked.**

Did Addie want to? Her quickening breaths, elevated heart rate, hard nipples, and damp panties screamed, fuck yes.

> **Addie: OK. Um, I'm interested in getting the tour. The full tour.**

> **Gray: Good to know**

> **Gray: While it's off limits…for now, you're more than welcome to check out my bedroom.**

"He wants me to…?" Her phone buzzed again.

> **Gray: Addie, you have my permission to explore**

"Oh, okay. He wants me to check out his bedroom. Cool, cool, cool."

To hell with dinner. Addie's curiosity about Gray's bedroom became her sole focus. She put her plate in the fridge out of harm's way, aka Minnie, and her phone buzzed with another message.

Gray: I wanted to show you in person…I didn't want to get into things when I needed to leave for work.

"What the hell's in his bedroom?" Addie muttered, taking a few steps down the hall toward the room under discussion.

Addie: You're sure you want me looking when you're not here?

Gray: I am

Gray: I meant what I said

Gray: I want you to make yourself at home

Addie: Okay. What if I wanted to wait until you're here to show me?

Gray: I appreciate the gesture; however, it's unnecessary.

Gray: It's my fault for not showing you today

Addie: Alright

Her feet propelled her the rest of the way down the hall until she reached a sliding barn door, the height of the wall in the same rich blue accented throughout the living room and kitchen, finding the bedroom door open wide enough for Addie to stick her head in.

So she stuck her head in.

Addie gasped. "Oh my God, it's...." She needed a better look and pushed the double-sided door open the rest of the way. "This is not what I expected. I...this is a dream bedroom."

A California king took up most of the wall across from the entrance on a raised platform. Covered in a cream comforter with dark blue sheets and pillows. When Addie entered the room, her bare feet went from smooth hardwood to a luxurious rug cushioning her every step.

She turned to her left to find the room extended into an open ensuite with a soaker tub, surrounded by a wall of windows and a view of the field and forest beyond. The vast shower took up the opposite wall, tiled on three sides with a glass front and two large rainfall spouts on opposite ends above. A shower built for two....

> **Addie: Your bedroom is like a sanctuary. It's beautiful. I'm impressed, Mr. Matthews.**

> **Addie: The ensuite is a dream.**

> **Gray: You can use it if you want**

"What?"

> **Gray: the tub, I mean, lol...it's supposed to be a clear night, perfect for stargazing.**

Addie looked up, staring at the sky through the glass ceiling. "Oh...oh, wow." To hell with multiple descriptors. One word repeated in her mind: Wow. Wow, wow, wow....

Addie: You want me to use your tub?

Gray: Oh, yeah. I want to imagine you there...

Addie leaned against the counter while her pussy went haywire. She hadn't been this turned on by someone in years. And all because a gorgeous, sexy, generous man wanted to imagine her using his spectacular tub. How can she say no?

Addie: Alright. I'll take a bath in your tub

Gray: Good girl.

Addie felt a flutter in her core. *Did she just have a* mini-orgasm *because Gray typed good girl?*

"I think I did."

Gray: Hey, I want to keep chatting with you, but we open soon, and I need to review a few things with the staff.

Gray: Have a good night, Addie. We'll talk tomorrow.

Damn, Addie wanted to keep chatting, too.

Addie: Okay. Have a good shift.

Addie turned off all the lights except the one above the vanity. She lit a few candles she found and set them on the counter, not wanting to take away from the starry night above her. She relaxed back in the tub and scrolled through her texts with Gray.

When she reached the end of their thread, Addie did something she'd never done.

> **Addie: I know you wanted to imagine it... I believe I can do your imagination one better...**

Addie opened her camera app and angled her phone, snapping a pic. She captured her legs from the tops of her thighs, peeking out of the bubbles down to the pink polish on her toenails, and without hesitation, hit send.

> **Addie: Until tomorrow**

"The ball's in your court, Mr. Matthews."

Chapter Fourteen

Gray

With Addie on his mind, Gray returned to his office when the club closed.

Did she settle in? Are Addie and Minnie getting along? Did she enjoy her bath...?

Gray picked up his phone to find he'd missed a couple of messages from her.

> **Addie: I know you wanted to imagine it...I believe I can do your imagination one better...**

A picture followed, and Gray almost swallowed his tongue. Long gorgeous legs ending in pink-tipped toes, surrounded by bubbles and candlelight.

> **Addie: Until tomorrow, Gray**

God, he wanted to hear Addie say his name... scream his name, while he made her come repeatedly.

Tomorrow can't get here fast enough.

love

Gray finished his morning errands, caught the earliest train he could, and walked through his front door by late afternoon.

His phone died halfway home because he kept staring at Addie's picture. The rest of the way...he used his imagination, after all.

"Hello?" he called, closing the door behind him. He almost said, 'Honey, I'm home.' Gray refrained, even if his renovated farmhouse embodied the word home for the first time. He inhaled, taking in the sweet scent surrounding him.

Addie baked for him?

The mouthwatering smell drew him to the kitchen, where he found cookies, brownies, and *Sweet Baby J* - cupcakes cooling on the counter.

Gray snagged a chocolate chip cookie, took a bite, and moaned. "Oh damn. This is the best cookie I've ever eaten." He popped the rest into his mouth and closed his eyes in ecstasy.

"That's quite a compliment. I'm flattered, but if you're not careful, you'll spoil your dinner," Addie said from behind him.

Gray spun to face her, caught in the proverbial hand in the cookie jar scenario. He swallowed. Addie giggled, coming closer, and the violet-haired baking goddess ensnared Gray.

"Isn't the deal baked goods for a home-cooked meal? You're not supposed to do both."

"You're letting me stay here, and I agreed to you making an occasional meal. I've got the rest."

Addie's gaze fixed on his lips. "You've got a little something...." Her gaze collided with his, and Gray forgot to breathe when she leaned in and licked the corner of his mouth.

"Mm. You're right. This is the best cookie I've ever made." Addie licked her lips and gave him a sassy wink.

The woman one-upped him from the café and drove him wild with lust. Gray wrapped an arm around her waist and tugged her close.

"All bets are off. No more teasing. And no more dancing around this chemistry sizzling between us." Gray cupped her face, his mouth an inch from hers. "Addie," he whispered.

"Gray."

He kissed her.

In fact, he downright consumed her, delving his tongue past her parted lips to collide and tangle with hers. She moaned and arched closer. Her sweet tits, with their hard nipples, pressed against his chest.

Gray pulled Addie closer until nothing separated them except their clothes. Lost in one another until the oven timer went off, they jumped apart.

"Wow." Addie clasped her heated cheeks and bit her kiss-swollen bottom lip.

Wow, is right.

Gray wanted to forget the food and devour her, except his stomach became the voice of reason when it rumbled, and he followed her around the island.

"Good to know the cookie didn't spoil your appetite." Addie bent over to take the dish from the oven, giving Gray an eyeful of her perfect peach of an ass. Damn, she's killing him with those black leggings clinging to her like a second skin.

Gray cleared his throat when she turned back, holding a steamy dish with a sultry smile on her lips. Well aware of her effect on him. "I hope you like lasagna."

"Love it." His voice sounded rough with desire. "Just let me wash up, and I'll be back in a minute."

While Gray had freshened up and calmed his persistent hard-on, Addie set the table with their dinner. "I hope you don't mind; I took liberties with your selection of wine," she said when he returned.

"Not at all. It's more fun to share wine and great food, anyway."

"You haven't tried it yet. What if you don't like it?"

"Impossible. Though...something is missing."

"There is?" Addie asked, looking at the table, searching for what she'd forgotten.

"Yup, let me go get it." Gray grabbed a pair of scissors off the counter and strode out the front door.

He hastened down the porch steps and rounded the corner of the house, searching for and finding the perfect bloom hidden amongst the ones yet to open, snipping the red rose for Addie.

When Gray returned and gave it to her, Addie buried her nose in the fragrant bloom, breathing in the sweet floral scent. "Mm...I love the smell of roses. Thank you." Addie pulled him in for a gentle kiss, not letting him deepen it. "Let me put this in water, then we can eat."

"You can use the small vase under the sink."

"Found it," Addie said, bent over with her head in the cupboard and her sweet ass in the air – giving him what he wanted.

"Fuck," he groaned, wanting to fill his palms with her fleshy cheeks. Gray stayed in his seat, concealing what he couldn't deny. How much he wanted Addison Carter.

"Sorry, did you say something?" Addie asked, taking the seat to his left. She put the little vase on the table between them.

"Oh, I said, this looks amazing."

"Thanks. Let me make your plate." Addie reached for the salad when he stopped her with his hand on hers. No time like the present to show Addie what it means to be his.

Gray took the bowl from her hand and held it over her plate. "May I?"

Surprised pleasure flitted across Addie's face. "Yes, please."

Gray enjoyed serving her, filling her plate with the food she'd prepared for them.

"Thank you," Addie said when Jasper set her plate down.

"No, thank you. It's been ages since someone's cooked for me like this."

A blush warmed Addie's cheeks. "You're welcome." She glanced at the counter and then met his gaze. "Sorry I went a bit overboard on the baked goods. I either bake or exercise when I suffer writer's block, and since there's someone to bake for, I enjoyed letting loose in your kitchen."

"Did it help?"

"Yeah, it did. I hit my word count and then some."

"Good-" he bit his tongue and stopped himself from finishing the sentence with 'girl.' Not yet. Gray cleared his throat and raised his glass. "A toast. You can bake for me anytime, Addie. Anything to help make the words flow." He winked. "Cheers."

"Cheers." Their glasses clinked, and they each sipped the merlot she'd chosen.

Addie's gaze filled with curiosity, and then she hit him with her first question. "So...you know about my longest relationship. What's yours?"

"Ah. The Inquisition."

"Well, nobody expects the Spanish Inquisition - nobody!" Addie said, giving him her most outlandish British accent.

They laughed, and Gray's tension eased. He wanted to be honest with Addie about his past, even if he wanted to leave his history alone. "A Monty Python fan. Good to know." Gray set his fork down and took another drink of his wine. "My longest relationship was six years."

"It didn't end well?"

"It ended with the return of the engagement ring I'd given her the previous summer. There are many sacrifices someone makes to have a partner in the military. Not everyone can handle it."

She covered his hand with hers. "I'm sorry."

He shrugged. "It happens. Everyone has their limits, right?"

"I suppose."

"The past is the past for a reason. My turn."

"Your turn?"

"Well, yeah. Fair's fair. You ask, I will answer. I ask, and you answer."

Addie gave him some good side-eye and said, "Okay." She took another bite of lasagna, and Gray became entranced by the way her full lips slid off the fork, imagining them wrapped around his cock.

He gave himself a mental shake. "Why'd you send me the photo?" Redirecting the conversation in the way he wanted it to go. Forward.

Addie picked up her napkin from her lap, patted her lips, and then sipped her wine, taking her sweet time answering. "Well, there are several reasons." She fiddled with the napkin, and a telltale blush heated her cheeks.

When it looked like Addie might share nothing else, Gray dropped his voice and asked, "Why'd you tempt me with the photo, Addison?"

Her baby-blue eyes went wide with desire and connected with his. "Because I wanted to be daring. I felt sexy and sultry using your bath, and I wanted you to know it."

Fuck. Gray. Was. Rock. Hard.

"You're all those things and more. I stared at your picture and stroked my cock, edging myself until I fell asleep." Gray turned her chair until her clenched thighs pressed between his. "Because the next time I come, it's gonna be in your sweet, fucking pussy I saw, peeking through the bubbles."

"Oh...fuck me," Addie whispered, leaning closer to him.

"I plan to, sweetheart. First, I want to get to know you, know your body, and make you come enough fucking times you lose your voice screaming my name."

Addie whimpered.

"Mm, dinner was fucking delicious, Addie. Thank you. If I don't stop, I won't have room for dessert, and that'd be a fucking travesty."

Gray pinned her with his gaze, making damn sure she knew he didn't mean the sweets lining his kitchen counter.

"We can't spoil your appetite." Addie bit her lip and shifted in her chair. Her clenched thighs and this little wiggle she did told him how turned on she was.

"No, we can't," he growled, thankful to discover he and Addie were on the same page.

Good girl.

Her lips parted with a gasp because he said it aloud. She tried to break the growing tension between them, rising to clear the table. He stopped her by grasping her hips.

"No way, Addie. You cooked this beautiful meal for us and baked treats I plan to savor later. Sit and enjoy your wine," he said, topping off her glass. "Let me take care of you."

"Um, wow, okay." Addie brought her glass to her lips, trying to hide her emotion over the simple gesture.

Damn. Addie's ex sure did a number on her. If he ever ran into the bastard, Gray would give him a lesson in manners he'd never forget.

Gray stood, taking their plates to the kitchen and loading them into the dishwasher. He made a detour on his way back to the table, stopping in the entryway where he'd dropped his messenger bag. Gray retrieved the papers Jasper gave him, along with a notebook and a pen.

He set them beside Addie and removed the rest of the food from the table, not wanting Minnie to get ideas about helping herself.

Gray said nothing, leaving them to Addie's curiosity, and he hid his smile when he heard the rustle of the papers a few seconds later.

He made up a plate of Addie's baked goods and packed the rest away. He set it on the table within reach and sat down. "Addie?"

Addie gave him a distracted, "Yeah?" Absorbed in the questions. Gray adored how she concentrated, because she now answered those questions with him in mind.

"Come here." He patted his thigh, showing where he wanted her to sit.

Her head snapped up, giving him her full attention. Still, she hesitated. "Oh, I-"

"Addie, I want you on my lap and in my arms for this conversation. Is that alright with you?"

"Y-yes."

Gray reached over and clasped her hand, tugging her from her chair onto his lap. He slid one hand over her thigh, settling it on her hip, and the other he brought around her back, tucking her against his chest. "Comfortable?"

"I am. I... you know, I don't remember the last time someone held me."

Fuck her dickhead ex.

Addie wiggled against him and gasped when she came into contact with his hard cock. "Oh."

Oh, is fucking right.

Then the temptress squirmed a little more, teasing him until he stopped her movements by increasing his grip on her hip. Gray didn't need help to deviate from his plan.

"You're sure I'm not too heavy?"

He growled in her defense over such an absurd question.

"It's...I mean...." Addie bit her bottom lip when her words trailed off.

Gray cupped her cheek and pulled her lip free with a gentle tug. "Addie. You make me hard." He emphasized how much by rocking beneath her. "You're sexy-as-fuck, and you turn me on. I want you in my arms like this all the time."

"Oh." She met his gaze. "Oh, wow."

She held the checklist in her hand. Gray reached over and pulled the notepad and pen beside him. "You filled out something similar for the club. This one's for me."

"I figured."

Gray picked up the pen and tapped the blank page. "The contracts I've done in the past remained within the walls of Decadent for the duration of the negotiated scene. I want more than casual or temporary with you."

"What kind of time frame are you looking at?"

Gray wanted to blurt, 'forever.' He considered his words, not wanting to scare her. "How about for the duration of your stay in this house?"

Addie sucked her bottom lip and bit down on the tender flesh, contemplating his offer. Worried about her hesitation, he added, "Open for renegotiation when you buy your house, of course."

"Okay," she said, giving him another tantalizing wiggle.

"Be still, or I can't concentrate." Gray scrawled a title across the page.

Addie and Gray's (Non-Legally) Binding BDSM Contract

Addie giggled, "Non-legally?"

"Well, it's not," he said, laughing too. Gray tilted her chin to meet his gaze. "It does still mean a lot to me."

"Me too."

"Good." Gray nipped at her lips, giving her a brief kiss. "We've already discussed this house. Are we adding other locations? What about Decadent? Do you want to go back?" Fuck, he hoped she did.

"Yes, I'd like to go back to the club. I didn't get the expected experience and want a do-over," Addie grumbled.

Gray chuckled and kissed the top of her head. "I'm glad because I have plans to make it up to you. Plus, Jasper sent me home a full membership for you, along with those papers. You can go whenever you like."

"What? I can't afford a membership."

"It's taken care of."

"What do you mean it's taken care of?"

Gray cupped Addie's face. "I mean, it's taken care of. Courtesy of Jasper and myself."

"Oh, um, okay. That's very generous, thank you."

"You're welcome. Speaking of Jasper, you know I stay at his place when I'm in the city. He has a basement apartment in his brownstone. Do you want to play there?"

"Is keeping it here and the club for now okay?" Addie asked, nibbling her bottom lip.

Gray tipped her chin up, making her meet his gaze, and then he tugged her lip free and soothed it with a kiss. "Addie, you never have to worry about setting boundaries. I'll respect them because I want to build trust and honesty between us."

"I may need you to remind me every once in a while."

"It'll be my pleasure." Then he gave in to his desire and kissed her again.

"Safewords. Want to use the club's standard stoplight system, or is there a specific word you'd like to use?"

"I'm good with the stoplight system. Green means all go, yellow means pause and discuss, and red means everything stops, correct?"

"Good. There'll be times when we may require non-verbal signals, like when your mouth's occupied." Gray growled beside her ear, picturing her sweet berry lips wrapped around him.

"We'll use the peace sign, a double tap, or a pinch. Everything stops if you do any of those actions."

"Okay." She shifted on his lap again, parting her thighs, nestling his cock between them.

He pressed his lips to her ear. "Are you imagining how I can occupy your mouth like I am?"

"Y-yes," she stuttered.

"Good girl."

Gray tapped the list Addie held with the end of his pen. "I want you to take your time and fill this out. Once you're finished, we'll review it together, and it will become part of this contract. I want to discuss your limits and anything else that may arise during the progress of our relationship. We can do this at any time. I'd also like to have a specific time to check in with each other every week."

Addie met his gaze and said, "How do Friday mornings sound? With Friday being your day off, we can have lunch and go over anything we may need to."

"Fridays work. I look forward to it," he said, adding it to the growing list of points. "Is there anything else you want to add?"

She read over everything he'd written. "There's nothing else I want to add right now."

"Alright then." He signed his name and handed the pen to her.

Addie and Gray's (Non-Legally) Binding BDSM Contract

Gray (the Dominant) and Addie (the submissive) agree to enter a D/s dynamic and contractual agreement for the duration of the submissive's stay. This contract is open-ended, amendable, and renegotiable whenever the Dom or sub believes it's necessary. Stone Barn Farm and Club Decadent are places where the Dom may take control.

Safewords. The Dom and sub have agreed to use the Red, Yellow, and Green. Non-verbal signals (peace sign, double tap, or a pinch) will bring the scene to an immediate stop.

We'll review safewords and non-verbal cues before every scene, the attached document, listing the submissive's hard and soft limits, and we'll review them when we try anything new. Our standing date is on Fridays *for lunch and a chat.*

Gray Matthews   *Addie Carter*

Gray lifted Addie to stand between his legs. "Ready for the rest of your tour? Because I'm ready for my dessert."

"Please," Addie whimpered.

"The wait's over, sweetheart. Come with me." He took Addie's hand and tugged her toward the basement stairs.

CHAPTER FIFTEEN

Gray

Gray stopped them at the bottom of the stairs, letting the anticipation build. His chest brushed against her back with each breath he took, and a cosmic current flowed between them where his fingers wrapped around her arms. He'd never experienced a connection like this before.

"Is it okay if I touch your hair?"

"Uh, yeah, sure, I don't mind." Addie glanced at him over her shoulder, a soft smile lighting her face. "Thanks for asking."

Gray's fingertips grazed her scalp, and Addie's little whimper went straight to his cock. He divided her hair into sections, telling her, "When you come down here to play with me, I want your hair braided," he said sectioning her hair into a neat plait down her back, then he secured it with the elastic from around his wrist.

"You can braid hair?"

"It's one of my many talents." His hands dropped to her waist, and Gray whispered next to her ear, "I'll also want you naked with your hands linked behind your head, waiting for my inspection." When she gasped, he let her off the hook. "We'll waive the protocol for now."

Addie shivered when he kissed her throat, then Gray leaned around her and unlocked the door; swinging it wide, he flicked the light on. "After you."

Addie glanced at him, then entered his playroom, turning in a slow circle. She took it all in, and Gray saw it for the first time through her eyes.

Now, Addie will know why Gray's obsessed with her hair color. It matched the wicked room before her.

Gray soundproofed the room and, under Martha's strict direction, painted the paneled walls a shade of violet and the recessed grooves black. The sconces offered warm, muted lighting strategically placed to highlight the room's unique furniture.

Martha may have designed it, but Gray had the final approval, and except for the plumbing and electric, he'd installed everything himself. All around him were items selected with a partner's pleasure in mind, *for Addison's pleasure.*

Gray's heart stuttered at the realization. Addie faced him again, her blue eyes sparkling with excitement and desire. He needed to slow his racing heart and get back to what he'd brought Addie here for.

Standing toe to toe with her, Gray tipped her chin with his index finger, putting her lips an inch from his.

Fuck, he loved how tall Addie was.

"Addie," he growled, nipping at her bottom lip. "This is the one time you get to explore, look, and touch everything in this room without restriction. Don't waste it."

"Yes, sir. What about questions?" She breathed against his lips.

"You're always allowed questions."

She smiled at his reassurance and pressed her lips to his. Then Addie slipped from his grasp and trailed her fingers over the supple leather of the spanking bench.

"Mm. I love the smell of leather." Addie said, giving him a coy look over her shoulder.

"Mm... something else we have in common. If you come to the barn, you'll find my workshop filled with the scent. It's where I craft the pieces I wear."

She glanced at the cuff on his left wrist and the thick belt at his waist. "You made those?"

"Yes. I made the restraints for here, too." Gray's eyes traveled over her curves, already crafting pieces for Addie in his mind.

"Impressive. It seems you have many interesting facets, Mr. Matthews, and I'm enjoying discovering them." She slipped around him, and there was that coy look again, making Gray chuckle. He was happy to follow her lead for now.

Addie grabbed the sides of the sex swing, rattling its suspension chains. "Does this require acrobatic training?" She asked with the utmost seriousness.

Gray crowded in behind Addie and placed his hands over hers on the harness. He rocked his lower body against hers, leaving no doubt about the effect she was having on him.

"Not at all," he said, lips next to her ear. "No special skills required. Whether I put you face down or have your feet in the air and your legs spread wide, you'll swing on my dick like a dream."

Addie gasped and wiggled her sexy ass against him. "Sounds fun."

"Fun?" he growled.

She giggled and slipped beneath his arm to open the cabinet, touching the tassels of his favorite flogger with reverence. "Did you make this too?"

"Yes. The other ones I purchased."

It pleased Gray that Addie zeroed in on the one he'd made amongst his collection. He pictured her tied to the spanking bench, restrained with the leather cuffs he would make for her, her back arching while he rained the flogger's tassels over her back, ass, and upper thighs.

"These implements are on the list, right?" Addie asked, dragging him from the illicit daydream.

"Yes, they are." Gray opened the drawers, showing her everything he had, and if there was something Addie wanted to try that wasn't here, he'd get it for her. "You won't find anything harsher than a leather paddle in there. I enjoy doling out a spanking or the dull thud of a flogger, turning a sub's skin a delicious shade of red. I'm not a masochist and prefer giving pleasure over pain."

"Lucky for me, since I enjoy receiving pleasure more than pain," she said, pushing the drawers closed after she perused each one.

"There's a fine line between pleasure and pain," Gray said, caging Addie against the cabinet. She turned in his arms and met his gaze. He leaned in and nuzzled the sensitive spot below Addie's ear. "It's a line I enjoy riding."

"Good to know." She kissed him and ducked beneath his arm, making another escape. Gray was enjoying every minute of this little cat-and-mouse game.

Addie stood near the end of the leather couch. Gray pictured her bent over the overstuffed arm with her legs spread wide while Addie's gaze darted to the stockade opposite.

"You're not ready for the stocks, sweetheart. It's on the list. Select it if you want to try it, but I'll warn you, it's not for the faint of heart, Addie. Though, the thought of you locked in it while I fuck you until you come on my cock and scream my name is something I'd like to happen."

Addie shuddered and whimpered in response while Gray closed in on her, done with the chase. Ready to capture her. "You ready for dessert?"

"Please, Gray...I need....."

"You're exquisite when you beg, Addie. Bend over the end of the couch for me and tug your pants and underwear to your knees."

Addie did what he asked, laying her upper half against the white leather. Addie pressed her cheek to the cushion, keeping her eyes fixed on him. She reached back and hooked her fingers into her waistband. She tugged her leggings and underwear down together, exposing her creamy flesh and glistening pussy, leaving them bunched at her knees.

"Good girl. Now put your hands on the cushion beside your head and brace yourself, Addie, because I'm fucking hungry."

Gray admired Addie draped over his furniture like she's made to be there. "Fuck you're beautiful."

"Please...please touch me, Gray."

He skimmed his palms over her lush cheeks and groaned, "Gonna do more than touch you, sweet girl."

Gray gathered the bottom of her top and bunched the material beneath her arms, baring her lacy bralette. "Pretty as it is, it needs to go. It's in my way." He leaned over and pressed his jean-covered erection against her ass; reaching beneath her, he shoved her bra out of the way.

He filled his palms with her gorgeous breasts, massaging them and teasing her nipples with his thumbs. They hardened beneath his touch. Gray tweaked them, pinching and tugging them until she whimpered and writhed against his cock.

Begging him with her body and her mouth. "Gray, please."

Gray nipped the shell of her ear and growled, "Keep begging for it, sweet girl. I'm going to make you explode so fucking good."

Gray let go of her breasts and stepped back. Addie whimpered and shifted on the arm of the couch. "Don't move," he commanded, grabbing a chair and setting it behind her.

"What are...?"

"Shhh...I'm just getting comfortable to enjoy my treat." Gray spread his legs on either side of her trapped ones when he sat. He gripped her ass, spread her cheeks, and admired everything in between. "Fuck. Your pussy is gorgeous and suffering from my favorite condition; dripping wet for me."

Gray pressed closer and breathed in her intoxicating arousal, unable to wait another moment to have her flavor on his tongue.

Gray licked her from her clit to her opening, driving his tongue inside her, tasting her sweet, musky flavor for the first time. "Fucking amazing," he groaned against her pussy.

He gripped her harder, spread her wider, and buried his face between her cheeks, worshiping and sucking every part of her, grazing her clit with his teeth.

"Fuck the baking, Addie. I want you naked and spread on my kitchen counter. I need to gorge myself on your sweet pussy every fucking day."

Addie did this giggle-whimper-moan combination thing when he focused on her clit. Gray sucked her sensitive nub past his teeth, flicking it with his tongue until she whimpered, "Gray, I'm going to...to...."

"Yes, Addie. Come for me," he commanded, ramping up his efforts until she exploded on his tongue with a long-drawn-out cry that ended with his name.

Gray licked and sucked her folds, lapping up her release while extending her pleasure. When Addie gave one last shudder, Gray surged over her and kissed her, letting her taste herself on his tongue.

"I'm not done with you yet," he growled against her lips. "You're going to come for me again."

"I-I don't know if I can."

Gray studied her flushed face and desire-filled eyes. "You can, and you will. What's your color, Addie?"

"Green."

"Good girl." He kissed her again, then slid back into his seat, dragging his clothed body over her bare one. He massaged her ass, spreading her for him to admire her dripping core. "You ever squirted when you've come?"

"No, never."

"Never say never," he said with a deep chuckle.

Gray dove his face back between her legs, working her into a frenzy with his lips, teeth, and tongue. He added his middle and ring fingers inside her, leaving his index and pinkie to press on either side of her clit.

Addie trembled, every muscle in her body tensing, her pussy clenched around his fingers, at once trying to keep them in and push them out, drawing closer to her next release. Gray replaced his mouth with his thumb against her clit, circling it faster and faster while he made a downward come-hither movement with the fingers inside her, pressing and rubbing her G-spot.

"Fuuuck, the way you tighten around my fingers, Addie. You're close, aren't you?"

"Y-yes."

"Is the pressure building?"

"Yes, Gray. It's...intense."

"Don't resist it. Let it build until you've no choice but to let go." He finger-fucked her harder and pressed down on her clit with his thumb. "Soak my hand with your cum, Addie. Come for me."

"Gray," she screamed. Her pussy clamped down, pushing his fingers free, and her liquid release splashed against his palm. Addie's body writhed and shuddered, pulsing with her orgasm.

"Yes, sweetheart. Such a good girl." He gentled his touch, kissing up the length of her spine until he reached her lips.

Addie groaned and murmured against them, "I've never experienced something like this...."

"If I have my way, you will. Every. Damn. Day. From now on."

Gray straightened her underwear and pants and settled Addie into the corner of the couch with an extra soft blanket around her shoulders. He gave her a water bottle and kept Addie in his periphery while he cleaned up. "Drink some more, sweetheart. I'm almost done here, then I'll take care of you."

Addie took a few more sips, then said, "You've taken care of me. What about you?"

"Give me a second." Gray threw out the used paper towel, washed his hands in the attached bathroom, and joined her on the couch. He held out his hand, and when Addie took it, he pulled her against his chest.

"Comfortable?"

"Mm, yes."

"Good." Gray kissed her temple and breathed in her sweet vanilla scent. "Has anyone put you first? Your needs? Your desires?"

"I- No...not even during my childhood. My parents kept themselves busy enough to forget their children who waited at home, and Barry...well, I've enlightened you on how our relationship went."

Gray rubbed soothing circles on Addie's back. "I won't ever treat you the way he did. I want to worship and treasure you. Giving you pleasure and fulfilling your desires gives me pleasure. I'll fuck you, Addie. Believe me, I will, but let me show you what it's like when someone puts you first."

"I...okay."

"You ready to go upstairs? I'll run us a bath. We can relax and view the stars together this time."

Addie tilted her head back and met his gaze. "Sounds perfect."

Gray helped her to her feet and walked her upstairs with a hand at the base of her spine.

With each step, his anxiety spiked.

Gray knew how he looked dressed or when he kept his pants on, yet he always experienced this unease when he got naked with a partner for the first time. His scars aren't pretty, despite his effort to cover them up, and he didn't want Addie to be repulsed by them.

Chapter Sixteen

Gray

"I still can't believe this is your bedroom. It's straight out of the pages of a boudoir magazine. Wait, is there such a thing as a boudoir magazine? Cause there should be."

"Not sure. Funny, Jasper said the same thing," Gray said with a laugh.

Gray tugged her past his bed, all too tempted to topple Addie into it and into the bathroom beyond.

He turned on the taps and lit the candles she had used the night before. He busied himself and avoided her curious gaze, which wasn't like him and something Addie picked up on.

Addie tugged on the back of his t-shirt, stopping his movements. "Grayson. Is everything okay?"

"Don't I seem okay?" he replied, trying to redirect.

Addie's hand moved from his shirt to his forearm, squeezing his tense muscles, sensing he was on the verge of spiraling.

Gray took a fortifying breath and turned to face her.

"Do you always answer a question with a question when you need to deflect?" Addie countered.

"No. Maybe...sometimes."

"What changed between here and the basement, Gray?" Addie's expression went from concerned to uncertain. "Do you regret what happened? This works both ways. You need to tell me if something isn't working for you."

Shit. He's fucking this up.

Gray held Addie by her shoulders, tracing the edge of her shirt along her collarbone with his thumbs; the motion soothed them both. "I regret nothing except the awkwardness of this moment," he said, again trying to deflect.

"I don't understand. We've already talked about what happens when I buy a place. I have no plans to stop getting to know you. What's this about, Gray?"

His chuckle sounded hollow in his ears. "How do I say this without sounding conceited or like a fucking tool?"

Addie's palms slid over his chest. "I promise you won't do either of those things." She glanced at the rising water. "The tub's almost full. Take a moment. I'll be right here when you're ready."

"Thank you." Gray kissed her lips, stopping the other words he wanted to say.

"Gray? The tub's almost full," Addie said again, breaking their kiss.

He wanted to say, fuck the tub and keep kissing Addie, but dealt with the taps all the same. Gray leaned against the counter and gripped the edge because he didn't want to appear defensive by crossing his arms.

"I'm aware of how I'm perceived by others. Approached by agents in modeling and film over the years. They called me flawless without ever seeing all of me."

Gray ran a hand through his hair and yanked on the strands. "I've learned the scars I carry are too much for some to deal with. Most of the damage I've covered with tattoos, and I know I'm making this a bigger deal than it is. I...." Gray shrugged, not knowing what else to say.

Addie stared at him for a moment. Then she whipped her top over her head, and her lace bra followed close behind. She tossed them both onto the floor.

When Addie yanked her pants and underwear off, Gray got his tongue working and asked, "What are you doing?"

"Getting naked. FYI, resistance is futile against my seductive attempts."

Gray snorted. Straight up snorted. Addie cupped her hand over her mouth and giggled. "Fuck, you're adorable."

"Look, it took me a long time to accept any kind of compliment, but that's not what this is about," Addie said, stepping into his space and bringing her beautiful body within reach.

Addie cupped his face and looked into his eyes. "I can't imagine what going into battle or putting your life on the line is like, and if you ever want to talk, I will be here to listen. I do, however, know what it's like to be insecure about parts of my body because of scars."

"You're beautiful, Addie. I want to map every dip and valley of your body with my hands, followed by my tongue."

"Says the guy who looks like he stepped off the pages of GQ."

Addie pointed to the faint silver lines on her cleavage. "When these first showed up, my classmates' teasing and ridicule ensured I covered them for years. Even after they faded."

"Your tits are fucking gorgeous." And he meant every word. "I'll destroy anyone who says otherwise."

"Thank you, but no destroying of others necessary." A blush heated Addie's cheeks, and his gaze followed her hands from her breasts to the soft curve of her stomach, where more silver scars covered the area below her navel.

"These showed up two weeks before Sadie's birth via C-section." Her fingers moved to trace the faint surgical scar above her mound.

"Can you believe I didn't rock a bikini until I turned thirty-five? I hid behind boxy one-pieces and t-shirts for these scars. I wasted years on others' opinions of me, letting their words eviscerate me for these. Not anymore."

This breathtaking, brave woman is baring her soul to him, and if his leg hadn't given out, he'd kneel at her feet and worship her. "What changed?"

"You know, I'm not sure. It didn't happen overnight. All I know is the fucks I used to give disappeared. Do things still get to me? Oh, yeah. Not superficial shit like perceived imperfections and people with unwanted opinions. Those stopped mattering years ago."

Gray rubbed a hand over his face. "Fuck, I'm an idiot."

"Nope. Uh-uh. You don't get to invalidate how you feel. I'm sorry your ex hurt you."

Gray leaned forward and pressed his forehead to hers, rubbing her arms. "Eh, she was just the first."

Addie cupped his face, and when Gray met her gaze, he saw a fierce warrior ready to battle on his behalf. "Who do I need to destroy?"

A weight lifted from Gray's shoulders. One he'd unknowingly carried for years. He wrapped the end of Addie's braid in his fist and tilted her head back. He met her lips in a fierce kiss.

When their lips parted, Addie gave him a saucy look. "How much of a rockstar am I for having this soul-baring conversation stark-ass naked?"

"Rockstar? More like a sex goddess. Are you cold?"

"No. Our water will be, though, if we don't move this to the tub."

"True." Gray expelled a deep breath. "Undress me, sweet girl."

Addie peered at him from beneath her lashes and, with a radiant smile, said, "There he is."

"Sorry, I got lost there for a bit."

"I'm glad I was here when you found your way back."

"Me too." Gray undid the leather cuff on his left wrist while Addie bunched his t-shirt in her grasp, dragging it up his sides. He lifted his arms, and she pulled it over his head.

"Well, now I know what it says."

"What?" he asked, finding her gaze focused on his chest.

She traced the letters with her fingertips. "The night I ran into you, the dim lighting and your leather harness obscured the words. *Carpe diem.* Seize the day."

Gray's breath caught when she pressed her lips to each letter. "Addie," he groaned.

"Take my pants off and leave my boxers. If you're going to be looking at my leg, I don't want you doing it with my dick waving in your face. He's eager to say hello."

Gray tipped his chin, acknowledging the staining bulge behind his zipper. "Let's get this part out of the way first."

Addie lowered to her knees and undid the heavy buckle of his belt. Gray pulled it free of the loops and set it on the counter beside his cuff. She tackled his button and zipper, keeping her gaze locked with his while she lowered his jeans down his legs and helped him step out of them.

"It's okay, Addie. I'm good. You can look."

Addie held his gaze a moment longer, then sat back on her heels and dropped her eyes to his bum leg while Gray kept his gaze straight ahead.

"I'm so sorry you got hurt, Gray. This Phoenix tattoo is badass. The artist used your scar tissue to build the flame, the ash, and the rebirth. Their artistry is incredible. Is it okay if I touch you?"

"God, yes." Gray dropped his gaze at the first touch of her fingers, shuddering when she trailed them over his upper thigh, along the colorful wings of his phoenix where the most damage to his leg was.

"Does it still cause you pain?"

"It's nothing I can't handle. The brutal rehab I went through made the surgeries look like child's play."

"How did it happen?"

"That story requires soaking in the tub and gazing at the stars. Come on." Gray helped Addie into the water.

"Lean forward, and I'll get in behind you." He removed his underwear and slid behind her, pulling Addie back against his chest.

Gray massaged her shoulders and arms, then linked their fingers, resting their joined hands along the tub's edge. Addie tilted her head, and he kissed her temple.

"Mm," she hummed.

"I can't disclose many of the details. Despite being out of the military, the missions I went on remain classified. Our task involved rescuing someone, and while we succeeded, our team got ambushed."

His grip tightened on hers. "One fucker tossed a grenade my way, and I didn't quite escape the blast. Shrapnel tore up my leg, and my artery got sliced. I lost a lot of blood. If Everly and West didn't get to me in time...."

"Oh...." Addie's hands roved his skin as she searched for open wounds where only scars remained.

He kissed her temple again. "I'm here. I'm good. West's the one who did my ink, and if he ever gets his ass back to the city, I'll introduce you."

"If he's accepting clients, I'd love to commission a piece."

Gray traced the flowers and hummingbird wrapping around her forearm. "You want more ink?"

"What they say is true. Once you get one, you want more."

"Oh, I know," Gray said with a chuckle.

They drifted into a comfortable silence, gazing at the stars above them, when Addie spoke again. "Your scars don't detract from your beauty, Gray. They enhance it."

Gray closed his eyes, absorbing Addie's words. "Sleep in my bed with me tonight?"

CHAPTER SEVENTEEN

Addie

Addie's eyelids popped open, and she sucked in a breath. The weight and warmth of Gray's arm around her waist registered, and his soft snore filled her ears. She expelled her breath with a silent whoosh and relaxed against the solid wall of man-muscle behind her.

She turned in his arms, wanting to observe him for a few minutes while he slept, doing her best not to wake him. Addie's attempt at being stealthy failed. Gray's dark eyes met hers when she faced him. "Morning," she squeaked. "Didn't mean to wake you."

"Mm, no, you didn't. I had the best dream last night, and to open my eyes to discover that it's true is fucking amazing." Gray kissed her forehead, and Addie melted into an internal puddle of goo.

Eek! Forehead kisses.

Gray's palms slid up and down her back and rubbed her tender muscles. One hand slipped below her waist, and over her ass cheek, then he squeezed, making her moan and arch into his impressive morning hard-on.

Yes.... Addie needed his big dick inside her.

Gray kissed a trail from her temple to her throat. "Mm, you taste so fucking sweet. I need more."

Addie squealed when Gray flipped onto his back, taking her with him. When she landed, she straddled his chest, her bare pussy pressed against his sternum, making them both groan.

After their bath last night, Gray dried them both, threw on a pair of briefs, and gave her one of his t-shirts to sleep in. It was long enough to brush the tops of her thighs, and he gathered the material at her hips; holding it there, he kept her pussy displayed for him while her arousal dampened his skin.

A flush heated Addie's cheeks, and she tried to rise onto her knees. "I-"

"Stay," he commanded. "I can feel how wet you are for me, Addie, and I'm hungry."

"You want breakfast? Now?"

Gray laughed, and the rumble vibrated against her clit, making her moan, and his grip on her hips tightened.

"After you grab a shower and dress, I'll make us breakfast. Right now, I need a little sustenance. Lose the shirt. Drag your sweet pussy over my chest and sit on my face. I want you riding my tongue while you drown me in your sweet cum."

Holy. Fuck.

This sexy man didn't keep his eyes off her, making her feel wanton and desirable. Addie tugged the ends of his t-shirt from his grip, dragging the edges between her breasts until the material pulled tight beneath them, her hard nipples visible through the taut fabric.

"Fuckin' sexy tease," he grumbled, making her giggle.

"I'll show you a tease." Addie kept pulling the shirt up between her breasts, revealing the soft undersides until she dragged it past her taut nipples, her tits bouncing when she flung it over her head.

"Fuuuuck. I'm gonna worship every inch of your body, Addison. Grab the headboard and sit your sweet cunt on my face."

"No one's ever talked to me this way." Addie rocked against him, so turned on she didn't even realize she did it.

"I'll stop if you don't like it."

She didn't want him to stop.

"What? God, no. I want more."

"Then get up here, and I'll give it to you."

"Yes, sir." Addie leaned forward to grip the top of the headboard when Gray sucked her right nipple in his mouth and grasped her left between his index finger and thumb. "Oh...," she moaned, arching into his touch.

Gray sucked harder, taking in more of her breast, and for a moment, she forgot all about sitting on his face while he teased and played with her.

"Fuck, your fucking tits are perfect. Come drown me in your slick."

"I-I don't want to suffocate you." She's soaked already and worried she might do it.

Gray let go of her breasts and put his hands on her hips. "What's your safeword?"

"Red."

"What do we use if our mouth's occupied?"

"Peace sign, double tap, or pinch."

"I'll double-tap your thigh if I need a breather. We're both going to enjoy this. What's your color?"

"Green."

"Then slide on up and sit on my face, sweetheart."

Addie shuffled over his shoulders, and Gray slid further down the mattress until she hovered over his mouth. He pressed his nose to the juncture of her thigh and breathed her in, making her shiver.

Holy fuck. This man is...wow.

"Gray," Addie moaned.

His hands gripped her ass, guiding her pussy to his mouth. He kissed her mound, then licked and sucked her folds; groaning, Gray pulled her even further onto his face. He made out with her pussy the way he did with her mouth.

"Mm... feels so good," Addie rocked against him. Gray's fingers dug into her hips, encouraging her movements. She gripped the headboard harder when his tongue circled her clit. "Oh, yes...please. Don't stop."

Addie cried out when Gray doubled his efforts, sucking her tender bud into his mouth. Her muscles tightened, and she rocked harder against him. "Gray, I'm coming, I-oh...."

He grunted his encouragement and sucked harder, nipping her clit with his teeth and sending her tumbling into a powerful orgasm, shuddering and riding his face like he demanded.

Addie gasped for breath, her pussy still fluttering with the aftershocks of her release. Gray stared up at her from between her splayed legs, a massive grin on his face, and his lips and chin shiny with her juices.

"Again, Addie," he demanded, tugging her back against his mouth.

"Yes." No one ever made her come like this. If Gray planned to ruin her for any other man, he's succeeded, and they haven't even fucked.

Gray finally let her slip into a satisfied pile beside him after four orgasms. *Four.* Double the promised two. Dang. This man knows how to go above and beyond.

Addie turned when the bed dipped. Gray got up and pulled on a pair of jeans. He left them undone, his erection straining beneath his underwear. She wanted him. Desperate to be filled by him.

"Hey...come here."

Gray leaned over, kissing her lips, letting Addie taste herself on his tongue. She sank her fingers into his hair and whimpered against his mouth, wanting more. Gray gave her one more soft kiss and stood back up. "What are your plans for today?"

"Well, I hoped I'd get railed by your enormous cock, but then you put pants on. I'm not sure what to do," Addie pouted.

Gray squeezed his straining erection. "You'll get this dick soon enough. Keep being a good girl and coming for me like last night and this morning, and I'll give you my cock. Let's wash up, and then I'll make breakfast."

He left Addie slick, swollen, satisfied, yet needy for more. She found so many things she liked and admired in him.

Gray's powerful, brave, passionate, commanding, sweet, and vulnerable. She'd never met someone layered the way he is.

The bathroom door opened, and Gray sauntered toward her, shirtless and still in his jeans, much to Addie's disappointment.

Gray leaned over and nipped Addie's protruding bottom lip when he reached her side. He sat on the edge of the bed and asked, "What's your day look like for real, Ms. Carter?"

She laughed. God, she appreciated someone who made her laugh. "Well, Mr. Matthews, after I get my word count in, I have a few social media posts to take care of and a few emails to answer. I'll finish later this afternoon. Why?"

A scratching noise came from the closed bedroom door. "One sec. I need to open the door, or Minnie will take great joy in scratching the shit out of it."

How dare a pussy of another kind act out because of perceived neglect? The moment Gray opened the door, the formidable furball jumped on the bed beside Addie.

"Hey, Minnie." She butted Addie's chin with her head, her rumbling purr filling the space.

Addie gave her a scratch behind her ears, then Gray put her back on the floor. "I'll get your breakfast in a moment. I need to finish talking to the lady first."

"Mrrrrrraaaaooooowww." Then she strode away with her tail swishing in the air.

Addie snorted. "It's like she understood you and told you your answer's unacceptable."

"It's the true give and take of our relationship. Since Minnie has made her point, I wanted to ask, how does going for a drive sound? Head out along the coast and stop in Stonington for dinner."

"Sounds great. I can't wait to check out more of the area. Oh, maybe we'll spot some for-sale signs. I'll make sure my phone's charged to take some pictures."

"Good idea." Something like disappointment entered Gray's gaze. Addie blinked, and it was gone. "How about you get your sexy butt in the shower? Breakfast will be ready when you're done."

Gray kissed her forehead and gave her ass a playful smack, the sheet providing minimal protection. "No dawdling, Ms. Carter. You've got a word count to hit."

He gave her a wink and left Addie to hop into the shower. She'd go upstairs and get dressed later. She wanted to prance around in Gray's t-shirt and nothing else.

CHAPTER EIGHTEEN

Addie

Addie's fingers paused on the keyboard. Her gaze drifted from the computer screen to the forest beyond. One week into this new living arrangement, and she's falling hard. Gray made it so easy for her to do....

On their drive the other day, he surprised Addie with news of his extra time off. Excitement filled her with the prospect of spending even more uninterrupted time with him.

Gray spent his days working in his shop, checking on her often to ensure she ate and stayed hydrated. Attuned to Addie's needs like no one ever has.

Thanks to Gray's attentiveness and Addie's flowing creativity, she plotted her three-book series and was now well into writing the first draft of book one.

Addie planned to send the first three chapters to her editor this weekend for some much-appreciated feedback. After finishing these self-edits, she did not want to send Cheryl a grammatical nightmare.

At the moment, she's having a little trouble focusing.

Each night for the past week, Gray coaxed orgasm after orgasm from Addie's body, demanding one more when she told him she couldn't. Only for it to happen moments later, she'd scream his name while waves of pleasure wracked her body, and she lay satisfied in Gray's arms.

So far, he'd restrained her to his bed with leather cuffs and silky rope, demonstrating the many ways to tie her to the headboard or four corners of his bed. Gray used his mouth, fingers, and toys to wring every release from her.

In all those times, Gray didn't come. He'd cup her face and kiss her lips, telling her, "Your pleasure is my pleasure." Neither had they gone back to his playroom.

How does one describe being satisfied yet frustrated beyond belief?

Fuck. Addie wanted Gray's cock. To the point, she began dreaming about all the ways he'd fuck her. She yearned for the taste of his cum. Wanted to be strapped to his spanking bench with the sting of his palm against her flesh while he fucked her hard from behind.

Addie rocked her pelvis, sliding against the seat of her chair, and clenched her thighs together. "Ugh, I'm so fucking horny. Which is insane because I've never experienced this many orgasms in such a short time."

She'd checked off everything she wanted to try on the list Gray gave her, and they'd discussed what she wanted – in great detail, yet Gray still didn't fuck her.

"What is he waiting for? Wait, what am I waiting for? To hell with this." Addie raked her fingers through her hair and twisted it into a braid down her back.

"If he can't take the hint when I beg for it every night until I lose my voice. Like, does he have the strength and stamina of a god?"

"Not of a god, no,"

Addie screeched and spun around, finding Gray leaning against the open doorway.

He pushed away from the frame and approached her with a sexy smirk. "I do, however, have the stamina of a Dom who wanted to take things slow despite already having you under my roof and in my bed. I'm also a Dom who puts the needs and pleasures of his sub above all else."

Gray tipped Addie's chin with his index finger, and her breath hitched when she met his intense gaze. "Have I neglected to give you something you need, Addie?"

She whimpered. "I-I need...."

"Do you need my cock?"

Addie's whimper amped into a moan. "Please, Gray. I need to be filled by you," she begged him. Then she took things one step further and lowered onto her knees.

Gray peered down at her and said, "I told you the next time I come, it'll be in your sweet pussy. Now you're trying to tempt me into stretching your pouty lips around my dick so you can swallow my cum?"

"Can't I have both?"

"Greedy girl," he growled, cupping his stiff length through his jeans. "I'm gonna claim every one of your holes, and since you're begging so nice...I'll take your mouth first. Undo my pants, Addison."

Addie shuddered with anticipation, moving her hands from her lap over his jean-clad legs. Gray's muscles rippled beneath her fingertips when she squeezed his thighs.

She glanced at Gray from beneath her lashes as she dragged her thumb over the hard line of his cock, straining against his zipper. Gray caught his bottom lip between his teeth, a look of intense desire on his face. "Mm...fuck, Addie."

She undid the button and pulled his zipper down, finding him naked beneath his jeans. Gray smirked. "I may have approached this moment with a plan. I want you, Addie. Touch me."

Gray's jeans hung low on his hips. Addie freed his cock and pointed it at her lips. She paused, raking her gaze over what she wrapped her fingers around. Veiny, long, thick, and uncut.

Is it too much to say Gray's cock is fucking gorgeous?

"Fuck no. I want you to describe in great detail how much you like my cock," Gray said with a wicked chuckle.

Well then.

Addie licked her lips and stroked her thumb over the tip of his cock, smearing the pearlescent drop of precum over the sensitive crown. Then she drew his foreskin back on her downward stroke, leaned forward, and sucked the head of his cock past her lips.

Addie moaned, sucking Gray deeper into her mouth, her tongue sliding over his length while his salty flavor coated her tastebuds. "Mm...."

"Touch yourself."

Addie locked her watery gaze on him while her hand slipped beneath the waistband of her leggings. Arousal slicked her fingers when she circled her clit. Her impending orgasm made her muscles tighten. She squeezed her thighs, trapping her fingers along with her pleasure.

"Fuck. I can hear how wet you are for me," Gray hissed. "Play with your clit, greedy girl." His hands moved to the back of her head. "Let me take over. You concentrate on making yourself come."

Addie hummed around him and dropped her hand. Gray held her head, working her on and off his dick like a fucktoy. The way he filled and used Addie's mouth made her wetter, driving her closer to her release.

Addie held on, wanting to wait for him. She slipped two fingers inside her pussy, finger-fucking herself.

"Fuck, I'm going to need a minute. You're so goddamn sexy. Show me your tongue." Gray gripped the base of his cock, rubbing the head against Addie's tongue. "Fuck yes. You're gonna swallow everything I have, aren't you, sexy girl?"

She nodded, closing her lips around his crown, sucking and licking his slit.

"Fuck, that feels good, but I'm going to need your words," Gray said, pulling free of her mouth.

"Fuck, yes, Gray," Addie gasped. "Give me everything you've got."

"My greedy girl. Open wide." She did. "Give me your tongue." Gray slapped the head of his cock against it when she did, flooding her mouth with more of his precum.

"Fuck," he groaned, then palmed the sides of her head and buried his cock past her parted lips.

Addie breathed through her nose and moved a hand back to his thigh.

"Fuck, sweetheart. You take my dick like you're made to," Gray praised, thrusting in and out of her mouth. "You're gonna make me come. Get ready, greedy girl. Make sure you swallow every drop."

Addie doubled down, humming and sucking him deep. While the pace of her fingers increased on her clit. The closer Gray got to his release, the closer she got to hers.

When Gray rocked forward, bringing her lips flush with his groin, the first spurt of his cum hit the back of her throat. The moment it did, Addie exploded on her fingers. His pulsing cock muffled her cries as they came together.

Gray smeared the last of his release against her lips. His hold on Addie's hair kept her still while he made sure she licked up every drop. "Such a good girl."

Fuck. Addie loved it when he praised her and called her a good girl.

Gray tucked his spent cock back in his pants and helped Addie to stand. "Remove your clothes and leave them folded over the back of the office chair."

Addie did. Quickly.

Gray cupped her jaw and ran his thumb over her tender bottom lip. "Now, I want you to march your sweet ass down to the playroom. I'm going to strap you to my spanking bench and fuck you."

She gasped.

Did he read her mind?

"No. You like to discuss your ideas with yourself. It's endearing and insightful."

Addie grinned. She didn't care if Gray caught her voicing her desires aloud, not when he was about to make them come true.

"Yes, Gray."

Chapter Nineteen

Gray

Gray whipped his shirt off, placing it on top of the neat pile of clothes Addie left on the chair. He followed her from the upper floor to the basement, not taking his eyes off her sweet ass until they stood at the playroom door.

"Hands linked behind your head. Feet spread apart," Gray commanded, tapping Addie's right foot with his, making her spread her legs wider. "Perfect."

He pinched her left nipple, testing her, and she rose onto her toes. "Don't move unless I tell you." He tugged on it again once she settled.

Addie moaned when he traded his fingers for his mouth, sucking her nipple, soothing the tender bud with his tongue.

"Beautiful girl, look how perfect you are for me." Gray stepped behind Addie, pressing against her back. He tugged and teased her other nipple while he slipped his left hand between her spread thighs.

"Mm...fuck, you're wet," he groaned, with his lips pressed to Addie's throat. "You're going to soak my cock the moment I get inside your sweet cunt, aren't you?"

"Yes...," Addie moaned.

"Get the door for me. My hands are busy." Addie lowered hers from behind her head, her finger trembling when she unlocked the door and pushed it open.

"Good girl." Gray tugged on her nipple and circled her clit, making her whimper, and walked them into the room without halting his teasing strokes.

"Please, I need to come." Addie shuddered in Gray's arms and halted when she saw the spanking bench bathed under the spotlight in the center of the room.

"Oh, did you believe what's about to happen is your idea? Sweet girl," he said next to her ear with a wicked chuckle. "I told you I'd give you every-thing you need. And right now, you need my cock. Don't you, Addie?" Gray asked, nipping the edge of her jaw.

"Y-yes. Please, Gray." He let go of her breast and wrapped his fingers around Addie's throat. His fingers kept a relentless pace against her clit, driving Addie closer to the edge. Then Gray stopped right at the moment she was about to explode.

Addie cried out with frustration.

"Patience, sweetheart. I want you strapped to my bench first," he said, guiding Addie onto it.

Addie rubbed her cheek against the leather and breathed deeply when she draped herself over the bench.

Gray trailed his fingers down her spine, making Addie arch beneath his touch. Then he gripped her hips and pulled her back until her pussy aligned with the end of the bench.

"Stay right there." Gray buckled a leather cuff around her left ankle, then her right, sliding a finger between her skin and the leather to ensure they weren't too tight.

Gray tipped her chin until her blown-out pupils met his. "You good, sweetheart?"

"Yes," Addie said, giving him a blissful smile. "Green, Grayson. Give me everything you've got."

His heart stuttered. He knew Addie meant here and now, but Gray wanted to offer her forever.

"I'll give you everything you can take, sweetheart." Gray kissed her lips, then moved behind her, where he bent and swiped his tongue through her glistening folds.

Addie rocked against his face, seeking more while he filled his mouth with her sweet, musky flavor. He needed her to come. Addie swallowed his release. Now Gray needed to swallow hers.

"I'll make this quick, sweetheart. Need the taste of your orgasm on my tongue when I fuck you."

"Please hurry," Addie panted, wiggling against the supple leather.

Gray landed a swift slap where her ass met her thigh. "No topping from the bottom."

"Sorry. Oh, god. Please don't stop, I'll be good." Gray did it again, and she screamed. "I'm close, please...."

"Fuck, I love how you beg me." Gray pressed two fingers inside her and pushed down on her g-spot while he sucked hard on her clit, using his teeth and tongue to send her over the edge.

Addie clenched around his fingers as the first pulses of her orgasm fluttered through her core.

Gray shoved his jeans off with his other hand and kicked them aside. He came around the front of the bench and held his glistening fingers to her parted lips. "Taste how sweet you are."

Addie lifted her head and sucked his fingers into the heat of her mouth, worshipping them the way she did his cock until she claimed every drop of her essence.

"Fuck. You're such a good girl."

When Addie reached for him, Gray tsked and stepped out of range. "It was neglectful of me to not finish tying your restraints." Then he buckled a set of cuffs around her wrists and secured Addie on the bench.

"Mm...please."

Gray stepped behind Addie once more, his gaze focused on her dripping pussy. "You like being held captive by me, don't you? Under my control, your anticipation builds, waiting for my touch."

Gray bent and nipped the fleshiest part of her ass, dragging his blunt nails up Addie's thighs to grip her ass cheeks. Then Gray spread her wide and devoured her.

Addie shuddered and writhed above him. "No, Gray. Please, I can't... I-I need your cock inside me."

"Addie," he growled, warning her.

"I'm not topping from the bottom. Promise. Well, not exact- I mean...I need you to fill me up. Please...please, fuck me, Gray."

"Mm.... When you say it like that, how can I refuse?"

His bare cock notched at her entrance, and Gray almost came like a teenager when Addie shifted her hips and sucked the head of his cock inside her wet heat.

"Fuck," Gray shouted, gritting his teeth, trying to control himself from slamming home.

When they discussed protection, Addie and he decided with no chance of pregnancy and clean bills of health, they agreed to forgo condoms. And thank fuck they did. Gray wanted nothing between them. "You ready?"

"Yes. Oh, fuck yes," Addie cried.

They both groaned when he thrust, sinking inside her to the hilt. "Fuck, you feel incredible."

Addie clenched around him while he rocked their world with steady strokes, bringing each of them closer to release.

"Yes. Fuck me harder," Addie demanded.

"Addie, we've talked about this bad habit you have of topping from the bottom," he growled, punctuating each word with a hard thrust. "You need something else, don't you?"

Gray smacked her right cheek with his open palm while he thrust his cock deep inside her.

"Yes!" Addie screamed, and her pussy pulsed around him. Then Gray smacked the other cheek, rubbing the blooming palm prints he left behind.

Gray pulled out and slapped her ass again while her pussy tried to suck him back inside. He gave her two more smacks, then drove his cock to the hilt.

Gray squeezed the tender flesh of her ass and asked, "You ready to come on my cock, sweetheart?" Close to letting go himself. Gray needed her to come first.

"Yes, yes, yes," she chanted. "Please, Gray." He reached beneath Addie and strummed her clit with his fingertips.

"There you go, sweet girl."

"I'm coming," Addie shouted.

"Fuck, yes." Her pussy tightened around him, pulsing and pulling him over the edge to meet his own release while he filled her with his cum.

Gray draped himself over Addie while they caught their breath. He held her close, pressing kisses along where her shoulder met her throat. "Amazing."

Addie let loose an adorable giggle-moan. "It's fucking amazing."

Gray wanted to remain buried inside her. His softening dick, however, had other ideas. He pulled out with a groan and freed Addie from her restraints. He then carried her to the couch, placing a soft blanket over her.

"Mm, thank you," she murmured.

Gray opened a bottle of water and handed it to Addie. "Drink and relax. I'll tidy up and then take you upstairs for a shower."

"Together?"

Gray leaned over and kissed her forehead. "Yes, together. Then, you'll grab a seat at the kitchen island with a glass of wine while I make you dinner. Then you can tell me how your book is going."

Addie tipped her head back and met his gaze. "I need you to pinch me and prove I'm not dreaming."

"Remember, I don't inflict pain to cause pain, Addie. I will, however, offer to remind you every day how real this is."

A blush heated Addie's cheeks, and she ducked her head when she answered, "I'd like that."

Gray trailed a line of kisses from her forehead to her ear and whispered, "If you're a good girl and eat all your dinner, I'll take you to bed and fuck you until you fall asleep in my arms."

Addie cupped his cheek and pulled him close, whispering against his lips, "How do you always know what I need?"

CHAPTER TWENTY

Addie

C an a girl ever have too many orgasms?

The limit does not exist!

Gray made Addie come until she lost count, rivaling a lifetime of orgasms. When she bought her house, how would she go back to not experiencing bliss every single day? Then, other intrusive questions made themselves known.

What if it takes too long to find something? Will Gray still want to date her? Or will the novelty of falling hard and fast wear off?

An email notification from her editor was the distraction Addie needed. "Minnie, what do you suppose Cheryl means by this?" The cat glanced at her, then returned to staring at the bird perched outside the window.

"You're no help. I'm going to find your dad."

Addie found Gray in the kitchen and plopped her laptop on the counter in front of him. "Is this good?"

'Addison, darling. Read the pages you sent. Let's set aside some time this afternoon to chat. I'll call you at 2pm unless the time doesn't work. Until then, Cheryl.'

Gray's brows furrowed as he read the brief email. Then he looked at her and shrugged. "It seems fine to me. I wouldn't worry about it."

Ugh. Doesn't Gray know by now she overanalyzed everything?

"Is it good or bad? She called me darling. It's good, right?" Addie paced the length of the kitchen island. "Though she calls everyone darling. She hates it, I know it."

Yes, she's a forty-year-old woman having an existential crisis.

Gray snagged Addie mid-pace with an exasperated chuckle and wrapped his arms around her. "I'm sure it's fine, babe." He kissed the top of her head, and she almost melted into a gooey puddle.

Those forehead kisses are one hundred percent swoon-worthy.

Gray held her tight, his palm rubbing circles over Addie's back. There's nothing 'almost' about it. She's one hundred percent a melty, gooey, marshmallow mess.

Tipping her head back, Addie met his gaze. "What if-"

"She won't. What you read to me the other night will make her laptop catch fire. It's good, Addie. Your editor is going to love it." Gray brushed her lips with his, ready to soothe and reassure her.

It's not the type of reassurance she needed.

Addie traced the seam of Gray's lips with her tongue, wanting to deepen their kiss. Gray nipped at her bottom lip and asked, "You need me to distract you until your call?"

"Please," Addie begged, already a needy mess.

Gray slipped his hand into Addie's hair and tugged, arching her neck, holding her right where he wanted. "I'm locking you in my stockade and making you come until you forget the meaning of the word worry, let alone what day of the week it is."

"Oh, god."

"God's not here, sweetheart. Say my name."

"Gray," she gasped.

"Mm. Downstairs now. Strip and wait for me in front of the door, ready for inspection. You have five minutes."

She squealed when Gray sent her on her way with a smack to her ass.

Addie made it to the bottom of the stairs in record time, kicked off her pants, and pulled off her sweater, folding them in a pile on the stool beside the stairs. With her hair braided, she got into position, spreading her legs and linking her hands behind her head.

She heard the muted sound of his footsteps on the main floor, pacing and staring at the timer she knew he set to count down her five minutes.

Addie stepped in front of the door, tilted her head back, and arched her body, posing for the camera. Five seconds later, she heard a growl reverberate throughout the house, and she didn't move a muscle when Gray descended the stairs.

Addie clamped her mouth, suppressing a moan when Gray's heat surrounded her. His upper body pressed against her back, and she registered the soft kiss of leather. He'd put on one of his harnesses.

Fuck. Yes.

Gray shoved his phone in front of her face, and Addie stared at her image. *Damn, she looked hot.* With her body arched, her eyes closed, and her lips parted. Her tongue extended; Addie begged with her body.

"You like to show off, don't you, sweet girl?"

Addie's fantasies over the years included exhibitionism, and lately, she pushed that boundary more and more. With Gray, she wanted to explore it even further. "Y-yes, I do."

His hot breath teased the tendrils escaping her braid, and then he wrapped his fingers around it and pulled her head back against his shoulder, pressing his lips to her ear. Gray's voice sent shivers of anticipation down her spine. "You need a lesson in what happens when you entice me like this."

Gray controlled some features in his playroom via an app, and when he unlocked the door and pushed it open, Addie found he'd set the lighting low while music played in the background. "Kneel there," Gray said, pointing to a cushion on the floor. "I need to get things ready for you."

Gray moved toward the stockade and removed the slabs of wood forming the leg, arm, and neck holes until one remained where she was supposed to get on it...um...in it?

"Of course, this isn't a traditional stockade. Not when the torture is your pleasure," Gray said with a sexy smirk.

He covered the head of a Magic Wand vibrator with a condom mounted where she'd sit and gave her a wicked look.

Oh....

Then Gray opened the cupboard and took out his leather flogger.

This is going to be intense.

Gray took Addie's hand and guided her to her feet. He tipped her chin and held her gaze. "Remember when you first saw the stocks? Imagined what it'd be like to be restrained in them, and I said it's not for the faint of heart?"

"Yes."

"What's your safeword, Addie?"

"Red to stop. Yellow to pause and discuss. Green to proceed."

"Good girl. Which one are you now?"

"Green, sir."

Gray helped her onto the platform, then slid the first plank into place, trapping her legs above her knees. He added a board to the middle, then one for her arms and head to rest.

Addie's breathing sped up, and Gray paused. "We don't have to go further than this, or we can stop altogether. Never forget, the power is always yours."

"I know, and I don't want to stop. Make me forget everything except how to scream your name."

Addie fit her wrists in the grooves and leaned forward to rest her neck in the center. Gray slid the last piece into place and flipped a latch to hold everything together.

"The latch is engaged for safety reasons. I won't lock it...this time," he growled beside Addie's ear.

Addie shivered when Gray slid his hand over the curve of her ass and gripped her flesh. "Sweet, girl. What have we discussed about you topping from the bottom?"

"Not to do it?" Addie dared to sass. The first smack of his palm sent a sizzle of electricity along her spine. "Oh...don't stop," she moaned.

Gray landed a smack against her other cheek. "You like these funishments a little too much, naughty girl."

"Sorry," Addie whimpered when Gray squeezed her tender flesh.

"I'm not sure you are, but I believe you will be." Gray reached below her, and with the push of a button, the still head of the Magic Wand came to life.

"Oh. Ohh... fuck," Addie cried out when he increased the vibrations. Then Gray picked up the flogger and ran the tassels through his fingers. Addie felt the first soft thud land across her upper back when he stepped out of sight, followed by another and another, warming her skin.

Gray shifted, and the flogger's trajectory became her ass and upper thighs. With the steady pace Gray set and the vibrations centering on her clit, Addie's body tightened, and a pulsing release slammed into her, radiating from her core throughout her entire body.

"Gray," Addie screamed, writhing within her restraints.

"Again," he commanded, sending her hurtling toward another release.

"Gray...."

By the time Gray filled her with his cock, Addie lost count of the times she'd screamed his name.

love

Always prompt, Cheryl called right at two. Gray sent Addie upstairs, giving her privacy to take the call. With a lingering kiss on her lips, he headed out to his workshop.

Addie expelled the breath she held and answered, "Hello?"

"Addison darling, how are you?"

"I'm good, thanks, you?" Her voice sounded hoarse. Addie winced and took a sip of water. It's surprising she can speak after all the screaming she'd done.

Addie glimpsed herself in the mirror. Thankfully, Cheryl didn't suggest a video chat. There's no way to hide how well fucked she looked.

Cheryl seemed oblivious to the rasp in her voice, or at least chose not to comment on it. "Never better, darling. I don't want to keep you. Let me cut to the chase."

"Rip off the band-aid. I can take it." Addie held her breath and braced for it.

Cheryl laughed. "No need for band-aid ripping. I loved the chapters, Addison. I have some suggestions to help with the flow going into the third act, along with some word cleanup and grammar edits. You'll find them in your inbox now, though there aren't many."

Addie expelled her breath with a whoosh of relief. "Wow, thank you. I don't know what to say-"

"You don't need to say anything, darling." Cheryl's voice filled with mischief when she added, "I don't know what kind of research you've done. Whatever it is...it's working. You sound happy."

Addie swore Cheryl said, 'whomever,' but she let it go. "I am happy."

"Good. Keep doing what you're doing and send me the rest of the book when you're done. I need to know how it ends."

"So do I," Addie said with a laugh.

"Well, don't keep us waiting. You're on a deadline, after all. Go over my suggestions, and we'll talk more. Chat soon."

"Bye, Cheryl." Addie hung up the phone and squealed, making Minnie jump from her lap. The cat gave her a disgruntled look and sauntered away. She wanted to find Gray and tell him the good news. Then she'd get cracking on those edits.

Addie patted her sex-mussed hair and adjusted her plan. Shower first. Then she'd find Gray to tell him the good news and maybe thank him for his thorough distraction job with some distraction of her own.

CHAPTER TWENTY-ONE

Gray

"G ray?" Addie called when he heard the barn door open.

"Back here," he said, shoving the leather collar under a stack of swatches right before Addie strolled around the corner with a bounce.

Addie twisted her hair into a damp knot, and her face glowed with a fresh-scrubbed look. She wore one of his t-shirts, which satisfied Gray's possessiveness with something he'd worn surrounding her.

She'd knotted his shirt at her hip, and her cotton shorts emphasized her long, toned legs.

He groaned when Addie pressed those luscious curves against his front and hooked her arms around his neck. "Hi."

Gray wrapped his arms around her and kissed her parted lips. "Hello to you, too," he said. "You're in a good mood. I take it the call went well?"

"It did. Cheryl likes where I'm going with the story. I do, too." Addie kissed him and nipped his bottom lip, and Gray liked how she teased him like she'd never get enough.

"I came out here to thank you for earlier. Although, your workshop is kind of distracting me." Addie inhaled a deep breath, humming while she let it out. "It smells amazing in here," she said, looking around.

It's nice to know the woman he's becoming more obsessed with each minute appreciated the leather smell like he did. Hell, Gray wore enough of it for it to be part of his natural scent.

This means Addie enjoyed the way he smelled a whole hell of a lot, too.

Addie wrapped her fingers around the double shoulder harness Gray put on to test the fit. He wanted her to test the rest of its capabilities, and his mind filled with the possibilities.

"This is sexy."

"It's not just for show. Want to learn what it can do?"

"What can it do?"

For an answer, Gray lifted Addie onto his work table while she held tight to the straps at his shoulders. He cupped her face and looked deep into her eyes. "Do you trust me?"

Without hesitation, Addie said, "Yes."

Gray picked up the leather loop beside Addie's hip and slipped her foot through, sliding the leather up her leg until it hooked behind her knee, doing the same to her other leg. With the quick-attach hooks, he secured them to the heavy-duty D-rings on his harness.

"Hang on." Gray waited until Addie gripped the harness tight, then stepped away from the table with Addie suspended against him.

He'd gotten the measurements perfect. Addie's cunt pressed against his hard cock. Gray shifted, and her heat seared him through his clothes.

"Oh," Addie gasped, biting her bottom lip. She arched her back, dragging her cunt against his covered erection. "Oh...wow."

Gray leaned forward and teased her lip with his tongue while his hands roved her body. "Mm...I can have you bouncing on my cock with my hands free to touch you everywhere," he growled against her lips. "You and I are going to have fun with this."

"I believe it." Addie rubbed against him some more, testing her freedom to move.

"What was I thinking getting you in this harness with all these clothes between us?"

Addie squirmed against him. "Let me down, and I'll have us naked in less than thirty seconds."

Gray set her back on the table and unclipped the straps. Then Addie jumped to the floor and unknotted his shirt.

"Do you do custom orders, or is this for yourself?"

"I sell some cuffs, collars, and leashes at the club's fetish shop. No one knows I'm the one who makes them. The harnesses I make for myself."

Gray caught the moment Addie's gaze landed on the female bust with a pattern he'd sketched and pinned to it. The sight was enough to distract her from getting naked.

"I've found inspiration to create for someone else recently."

Gray caressed Addie's body while she melted against him. "To get it right, I'll need exact measurements."

Addie smirked and slipped from his arms to get a closer look. She bit her lip and glanced at him over her shoulder. "You want to make something for me?"

Gray captured her in his arms again, and they studied his sketch.

"I want to design harnesses, straps, and cuffs for you. Dress and restrain you in leather I've cut and stitched. This piece is a corset vest with buckles to do it up."

Gray traced his fingers along her throat, his lips pressed to her ear. "I can picture you in one of my white dress shirts, braless, while it hugs the undersides of your breasts and cinches your waist."

He ground his aching cock against Addie's ass. "Fuck. The idea of parading you around the club in it is making my cock even harder."

"I like the idea of being a muse for you since you inspire me." Addie turned and gathered his t-shirt around her waist. "I mentioned fixing the 'too much clothing situation.'"

Addie whipped his shirt over her head and said, "You better get my measurements because I can't wait for us to do all those things."

She stood in nothing except a white lace bra and those cute-as-fuck shorts. Those needed to go, though. Gray pushed them over her hips, revealing the matching lace thong when they dropped to the floor. He gripped her ass and her onto his worktable.

"Hm, I'm enjoying all this manhandling you're doing. I've always wanted to be manhandled," Addie giggled.

She leaned in for a kiss, and Gray pushed her thighs apart, allowing him to get nice and close. "Anytime you want to be manhandled, you let me know," he said against her lips, then deepened their kiss, sliding his tongue against hers.

Minutes or hours later, when they came up for air, Gray reached around Addie to grab his measuring tape and the pad of paper he kept nearby.

"Raise your arms." He wrapped the tape around her torso, grazing her nipples when he brought the ends together.

"For the record, this isn't how I take measurements. With you, I enjoy turning something mundane into a naughty game. The kind which end with you coming around my cock, making us both winners."

Addie traced his lips with her fingertips. "No one's ever spoken to me the way you do. I've read many romance novels where the MC excels at talking dirty. I never knew how much I wanted it until you gave me a taste."

"Anytime I can give you something you've missed out on, something you crave, I'm going to give it to you, Addie."

Gray tugged her forward with the tape and pressed his lips to hers in another searing kiss, leaving her breathless while he noted the measurement and moved on to the next.

"Tease."

Gray chuckled. "It's called foreplay and anticipation. You know I'll make it worth your while."

"I know. It's why I can't wait." Addie dipped her fingers beneath the bottom of his t-shirt and trailed them over his abs. Gray captured her wandering fingers, keeping her from going further. He wanted to ask her something before they got carried away.

"Do you want to go to the club tomorrow night? I'm back to my regular shifts in a few days and wanted to give you the tour I owe you. We can go to dinner, then I'll show you around Decadent. We can play and spend the night in the city."

"It sounds perfect, but I can't stay the night. I'm viewing houses with Richard on Sunday. He's got three properties to show me, and we're supposed to meet at ten to view the first one."

Right. Shit.

Gray blocked out the whole 'Addie's staying with him temporarily while she searched for a place to buy.'

They'd spent all this time in easy, kinky, sexy domestic bliss. Naturally, like they'd known one another for years. Gray wanted to do this forever. Did Addie feel the same?

Can Gray ask her to forgo buying a home and make this arrangement permanent?

He didn't, offering an amendment to the suggested night out instead. "How about I drive? We can have dinner at seven, hit the club by ten, and return to the farm by two. Gives us plenty of time to have fun and still get a reasonable amount of sleep."

"Um, okay. If you're sure."

"I'm sure."

"What about Minnie? Will she be okay by herself?"

Gray laughed. "I love the way you worry about her. Minnie will be fine, I swear. She stays on her own when I'm at work. I'd bring her to the city except Jasper's allergic, and to keep him from sneezing to death, Minnie stays here."

Addie smiled, and Gray swore the room got brighter. "Well, if Minnie's good, I'd love to go."

Gray noted her last measurement, then popped the button on his jeans and leaned in close, growling next to her ear, "Time to show you what this harness can do."

Addie shuddered when he hauled her off the table and into his arms.

CHAPTER TWENTY-TWO

Addie

When Gray finished giving her the fuck of her life – who was she kidding? Each time they had sex became the fuck of Addie's life.

Still slick with sweat and contemplating another round of the best sex ever, Addie froze. "What am I going to wear to the club?"

Gray pulled the t-shirt over her head, covering her upper body. He tugged on the hem and pulled her close. "Can I take you shopping?"

Skeptical. Addie regarded him from beneath her lashes. "Let me get this right. You want to take me shopping and wait while I try on multiple outfits until I find the perfect one?"

His arms tightened around her waist, and Gray trailed kisses along her jaw until he nipped at her lobe, making her shiver. "Yes, that's what I want to do. If you promise to model every outfit for me. I bet it will be hard to choose just one. Which means I'll have to buy you more."

What girl is going to say no to that?

Not this girl.

Gray rocked against her, pressing his thickening erection against her hip, making her moan. "You're going to ruin me for anyone else."

Addie bit her lip, but it was too late to stop her admission.

Gray pulled back and stared deep into her eyes. With a confident smile, he said, "Goals, Addie. It's goals."

Addie hoped like hell that this kind of happiness would never go away.

love?

When they arrived in the city, Gray parked in Jasper's drive and showed her around the basement apartment.

Then Gray took her shopping.

Not to a department store like Barry did, where he'd complain if they didn't look at something he wanted.

Nope.

Gray took her to a fancy Fifth Avenue boutique with a personal stylist and a gorgeous private fitting room. Where Gray lounged in a wing-back chair, looking sexy-as-fuck, waiting for Addie to model every piece he and the stylist selected.

Is she living out her rom-com movie fantasy right now?

Gray chose everything from her four-inch heels to the sexy, dark blue, matching bra and panty set that caressed her skin beneath the black vegan leather capris and the dark purple silk wrap blouse displaying her cleavage.

Or 'perfect tits,' as Gray growled, with his face buried between her breasts when the stylist left them alone.

Addie never felt sexier.

Gray told her how gorgeous and beautiful she was each time Addie opened the fitting room door. It took her decades to find the confidence she now has, and Gray's praise did something to her, building her up even more.

A giver all her life, Addie never knew what it was like to receive someone's undivided attention, someone who put her first until now.

Gray cherished her the way a heroine in a romance novel is, and until she walked smack dab into him, Addie never knew men like him existed.

Dinner was amazing. Gray took her to an exquisite French restaurant, satisfying their need for food, and now, a hunger of a different kind simmered between them as they made their way up the steps to Decadent.

"Nervous?" Gray asked, his lips pressed close to her ear.

Addie glanced at him. Gray kept a hand at the base of her spine, and she relished his quiet possessiveness and leaned into his touch. "Not in the least."

He pressed a kiss to her temple. His lips fired up her nerve endings, making goosebumps rise on her skin, and her nipples pucker into hard points.

He chuckled. "I am enjoying your eagerness. The night's young and full of possibilities."

"Not that young."

Over the last week, Addie wrestled with the big climactic scene in her novel where the female lead gets claimed by the male lead in a delicious display of praise and degradation in front of an entire club full of people.

Addie wanted to write it from the heroine's perspective to capture their emotions and experience of pushing their boundaries and daring to put themselves on display.

No author needed to go to such extremes for authenticity in their novels. It's not like she wrote murder mysteries. She'd never commit a murder to tell a great story.

Yet, being taken in front of others was something she wanted to experience personally.

Addie tugged on Gray's arm. "Have you ever claimed someone in public?" She didn't pay attention to their arrival in the lobby nor how they stood by Jasper and the stunning woman who checked her in at guest services the last time she came.

That is until Jasper cleared his throat, and Addie's head whipped toward them.

"Uh, Addie, you remember Jasper, and I don't believe you've met Kari Davidson," Gray said with amusement.

Oh. Shit.

"Um, hello."

Jasper's smile looked slightly strained, while Kari's smile grew to full-on megawatt status when she introduced herself. "Addie, it's a pleasure to meet you. Loved your book. Can't wait to read more from you."

Kari's enthusiastic greeting didn't quiet the echo of her curious question. "Oh, thank you. Sorry about blurting that out. It's an author-related inquiry," she said, over-explaining and praying the soft lighting hid the blush blooming from her boobs to her cheeks.

"Oh, yeah? Now, it makes me want to read your next book even more. Nothing like a possessive alpha staking his claim in front of a consenting crowd; am I right?"

Wait, what?

All eyes and surprise turned to Kari, who extricated herself from the situation with a wave. "I'm going to check these guests in. Fantastic to meet you. Jasper's right, Gray, she's perfect for you," Kari gave Gray a sassy wink, then strutted away.

"Brat." Addie heard him mutter, and she giggled despite the surreal interaction.

Jasper straightened his suit jacket. "Addison, it's a pleasure to have you back at Decadent. Please enjoy your night."

The smile he gave them didn't quite reach his eyes. "I'll talk to you both later. I need to check in with the staff." Jasper backed away and disappeared behind the double doors.

"Did I say something wrong? I'm sorry if my question isn't appropriate."

Gray sighed. "It's fine. And no, I've never done it, but...."

"Jasper has." Addie finished coming to her own conclusion.

"Yup," Gray said, popping on the p.

"Ah... that explains his intense 'I'm taken' vibes. Is his partner here?" Addie searched the people streaming into the club, looking for someone she'd never seen.

"Jess isn't here. It's...complicated."

"No doubt."

Gray held out his hand for her to take. "Come on. I'll take you to my office, and you can store your belongings. We can also discuss your desire to be claimed."

Addie linked her fingers with his, and Gray tugged her to a door where he used his key card to gain access. It led to a hallway and stairs leading to the top floor.

Gray pinned her to his office door the moment they stepped inside. His forearms bracketed her head, and his nose trailed along her throat, breathing in her scent and making Addie shiver.

"I memorized every single item you marked on your list. This isn't just for research, is it, Addie?" Gray pulled back enough to meet her gaze, his dark eyes missing nothing.

"No, it's not. I want every person in here to know I'm yours."

Gray cupped her face, keeping her gaze locked with his. "Are you? Mine?" Their breath entwined, and his lips teased hers with each word he spoke.

"Yes...I'm yours."

He groaned and pressed his mouth to hers in a searing kiss. His tongue skated across the seam of Addie's lips, demanding entrance. Which she happily gave.

Gray wrapped her hair in his fist, crowding Addie against the door until no space remained between them, and her curves molded to his rock-hard body.

He tugged on Addie's hair, separating their lips enough for him to whisper, "Good, because I'm yours."

Addie gasped, and Gray caught the sound when his mouth crashed against hers.

CHAPTER TWENTY-THREE

Gray

Gray pressed his forehead to Addie's, letting their heart rates calm and their breathing slow. Declarations of love formed on his tongue, seconds from being blurted if he didn't rein it in. *It's too soon.*

Isn't it?

Instead, Gray circled back to her original question.

"About your curiosity and need for realism in your book...while I want to give you the experience you deserve, it also takes planning and discussion. So I want to offer a compromise." There's no way Gray wanted Addie to think he didn't want her or what she proposed.

Addie arched a brow. "Oh, yeah? I'm open to negotiations."

Fuck, he loved her spirit and confidence. *There's that sneaky word love again.*

"Wait. Let me find out if the room I have in mind is available first." Gray offered her a seat in the chair across from his desk, noting the tremble in her legs.

He picked up the receiver on his desk. "Tilda, it's Master M." He kept his eyes on Addie and smirked when her gaze widened. *Ah, she forgot what he goes by here.* "Is the glass room free for the next while?" His smile widened at her answer.

"Perfect. No...mark it booked for the night. I'm not sure how long we'll be. Let Master Z know we'll be there soon. Thank you."

Gray dropped the receiver into its cradle and raked his gaze over Addie. Fuck, she took his breath away.

She'd done her makeup sultry and smoky-eyed. A vision of Addie on her knees with mascara tears running down her cheeks, taking Gray to the back of her throat, filled his mind.

"Gray?"

"Hm?" He reckoned it was not the first time Addie said his name.

"Sorry." Gray dropped into the chair beside Addie, capturing her left hand in his; he kissed her knuckles and gave her a devilish smirk. "I'm visualizing what I want to do to you tonight. Can you repeat the question?"

Addie moaned, frustrated by Gray's teasing strokes. "What's the glass room?"

Gray met Addie's curious gaze. "Did you notice the spot above the dance floor with a blacked-out section of ceiling lower than the rest?"

"Yeah. There are strobe lights along the edges. Is it a light show or something?"

Gray chuckled. "It's something. While it's blacked out now with the press of a button, whoever's inside will be visible to everyone below."

"Oh, um, okay." Addie's breath quickened. Gray flipped Addie's hand over and trailed kisses over her wrist. With his unwavering gaze pinned to hers, he held nothing back.

"I want to make you come again and again. When I fuck you, everyone will see how beautiful you are and how perfect we are together," Gray said, getting closer to making a declaration of another kind.

A whimper escaped Addie's parted lips. "Please, Gray. I want it. I want it all with you."

Gray leaned back and whipped his shirt over his head. "Everything, sweetheart. I'll make you feel fucking phenomenal." Gray promised, raking his gaze over her. "Everyone will know you're mine."

Gray got up, pulled open the door to the cupboard in the corner, and took out his favorite leather harness. The same one he wore the night he met Addie.

He slipped it over his shoulders and buckled each side above his pecs, tightening the straps until the leather molded to his body.

Gray smirked when he heard Addie mumble, "Fuck, that's hot."

He pulled Addie from the chair and into his arms. She gripped the leather, pulling him close. Gray cupped her face and stared into Addie's desire-filled eyes. "Glad you think so."

Gray gave her a heated kiss, making them both groan when he pulled away. "Leave your purse and shoes. You won't need them where we're going, and they'll be safe here."

Once Addie set her things aside, Gray locked his office behind him and stopped by the railing.

"Jasper and I always end up here during the nights we work together."

"You and Jasper have a strong relationship. I like that. Shows what kind of person you are."

Gray tucked Addie against him, caging her between him and the railing. He put his lips to Addie's ear and whispered, "And what kind of person am I, Addison?"

Addie turned her head and looked at him over her shoulder. "The kind I'd want forever with." She looked out over the club again. "The art lining the walls is beautiful."

Addison did not just do a complete one-eighty after dropping that little bombshell?!

Yet, Gray answered, "They're from Jasper's private collection."

"The portrait below us is stunning."

"He hangs one particular photographer's work below his office window. It's a running joke amongst the staff, and Jasper's under the impression no one knows who the couple is."

"Who are they?"

"Jasper and his wife, Jessica. He never displays one's showing their faces. He keeps those for home, but everyone knows it's them."

"Huh. You weren't kidding when you said it's complicated."

"Yeah, and they're the only ones who can uncomplicate it."

The opening notes of 50 Cents' Candy Shop filled the club and the lull in their conversation. A seductive smile spread across Gray's face when the crowd on the dance floor grew, sensing something monumental was about to happen.

And they'd be right.

Gray sent a message to the house DJ earlier to cue up his favorite playlist. He linked his fingers with Addie's and tugged her from the railing.

"What-?"

"Come. It's time. Time for me to claim you," he said, kissing her knuckles.

Gray led her across the walkway to the club's private rooms, where a dark and handsome man in a leather vest with impressive tattoo-covered muscles greeted them.

He let go of Addie's hand to grip Zane in a backslapping man-hug. "Good to see you, Z."

Zane grunted, "You too."

Gray didn't miss when Zane's gaze shifted to Addie as their hug ended. He stood beside her and placed his hand against the small of her back. Zane tracked the movement until understanding lit his gaze.

That's right. Mine.

"This is Addison."

Zane dipped his chin toward Gray and put more space between himself and Addie.

Smart man.

"Good evening, Addison. Are you entering the private rooms of your own free will?"

Addie didn't hesitate, nestling into Gray's side. "Yes."

Zane gave Addie one more assessing look, prompting an uncontrollable growl from Gray. When Zane stepped back with his hands raised in surrender and a conspiring smile on his lips, Gray knew his friend was fucking with him.

"Understood. You have a good night then," Zane said, giving Gray a knowing look.

"I'm glad you do, and we will."

"Don't forget this." Zane handed Gray the remote to control the room's features.

"Thanks." Gray slipped the remote into his back pocket and guided Addie toward the room at the end of the hall. The one which allowed guests to put on a variety of shows.

The glass room's about to go live.

When the opening lines of Pour Some Sugar on Me blasted through the sound system. Gray held the door open for Addie to precede him inside.

CHAPTER TWENTY-FOUR

Addie

Addie's heart rate sped up when the door clicked shut behind her, dulling the sound of the classic eighties hit. Her gaze jumped about the room, taking in the couches and cozy loveseat lining the far wall. Where on the other side, two St. Andrew Crosses stood.

Did Gray plan to tie her to one?

Then her eyes landed on the single object in the sunken center of the room, answering her silent question. Gray's not tying her to a cross....

Gray captured her chin, drawing Addie's eyes from the leather-padded sawhorse. He tilted her head until she met his dark, intense gaze. "Do you trust me?" he asked.

"Yes."

"Then strip."

Addie didn't hesitate, untying her blouse and slipping it from her shoulders. Gray took it from her hand and hung it on a hanger in a cubby to her left, doing the same with her pants when she removed them.

"That's enough."

Addie froze with her fingers on the clasp of her bra. Gray leaned in close, his lips next to her ear, sending a shiver down her spine. "I'll be the one to remove those. Keep your hands by your sides. I need to select a few things."

She heard him open and close cabinets and drawers. Then Addie's breath caught when Gray stepped close behind her and whispered, "Close your eyes."

Addie's lashes fluttered shut, and she shivered when something silky trailed up her arm and over her collarbone. "Do you remember your safewords, Addison?"

She swallowed, keeping her eyes closed like Gray asked. "We use the stop light system, sir. Green is good to go. Yellow is to pause and discuss. Red stops everything."

"Good girl."

"And your non-verbal cues?"

"Peace sign, double-tap, or a pinch will stop things if my mouth is otherwise occupied," Addie answered with a hint of sass.

Addie's sass turned to desire when Gray gripped her ass and squeezed. "Naughty girl," he said with a nip to her lobe. "Color?"

"Green, sir." The moment the words passed Addie's lips, the silk covered her eyes, and Gray tied the ends behind her head. Then his fingers trailed down her neck, along her spine, until he reached her bra. The band tightened and went slack when he slipped it off her body.

Gray wrapped an arm around Addie's waist and pulled her back against him. His hands cupped her breasts, massaging her flesh while he rolled her nipples between his fingers. She moaned and rocked her ass against his erection.

With one more teasing twist, Gray let go of her breasts and stilled her grinding by placing his hands on her hips. "Patience," he growled.

Addie jumped when Gray wrapped a leather cuff around her wrist, catching her off guard.

"Are you alright, Addie?"

"Yes. You just startled me." Addie inhaled a steadying breath, taking in Gray's scent, the alluring familiarity calming her. "Mm."

Gray spun her around and moved her hands to his shoulders. "I don't want you to lose your balance while I take these off."

His fingers skated along the edge of her panties, hooking them beneath the waistband. Gray tugged them down her legs until she slipped them off her feet. Naked except for the leather cuffs and blindfold.

"You're fucking gorgeous, Addie. I need to touch you."

"Please, Gray."

Addie dripped with arousal when Gray slipped his fingers between her folds, slicking his fingers and strumming her clit, taking Addie from zero to her first orgasm in seconds. "Oh, fuck. Gray, I'm coming," she cried.

"Such a responsive, sweet girl," Gray praised her, slipping his fingers inside her and prolonging Addie's release. "You're going to come for me all night, aren't you?"

Thank goodness Addie still held onto Gray's shoulders. That and the hand between her legs is what's keeping her upright. "Yes... all fucking night."

"That's it, baby. Ride it out," Gray cooed while his fingers curled inside her, and his thumb kept up a steady pressure on her clit. Addie climbed toward her next orgasm until Gray pulled his hand from between her thighs, leaving her...on the precipice.

Addie cried out in dismay over the unjust act.

"Hold on a little longer, sweet girl. Your next orgasm is gonna be on my tongue." Then she heard the distinct sound of Gray sucking her arousal from his fingertips.

"No. Don't make me wait," Addie pleaded, squeezing her thighs together, looking for more friction to send her into another release.

Addie rose onto her toes and let out a squeak when Gray's palm connected with her left ass cheek. "Keep your legs apart, naughty girl."

"Yes, sir," Addie grumbled, doing what he demanded.

"Better." Gray took her hands and guided Addie a few steps forward. "There are six stairs below you. Ready, Addie?"

Addie took a deep breath, releasing it in a slow, steady exhale.

Is she ready for everything?

"Make me yours, Gray. I want it all."

"And I'm going to do my damndest to give it to you, baby," he said, helping her down each step. "There we go. Walk with me for ten more steps, and you'll be right where I want you."

Addie counted in her head, reaching ten when Gray told her to stop. He let go of her hands, and then his palm gripped the nape, bending her until her chin rested on the padded leather. "Keep your head there and extend your arms."

He gripped her left hand and attached the cuff to one side, doing the same to Addie's right, keeping her restrained at a ninety-degree angle, making her breaths come faster.

Gray traced her cheek with his knuckles, then grazed her bottom lip with his thumb. She tasted the salt of his skin with the tip of her tongue and moaned.

"What's your color, Addie?"

She needed more, this time sucking his thumb into her mouth, only letting go to answer, "Green, sir."

"There's my girl." Gray's hands skimmed over her body, keeping them connected.

Addie drew up on her toes when Gray dragged his blunt fingertips down the backs of her thighs and pulled them apart. "Spread those legs, baby. I want everyone to get a look at your dripping pussy."

She shuddered in her restraints and widened her stance further.

"Such a good girl for me," he said, spreading her arousal over her mound.

"More, Gray...I need more."

Gray leaned over her, pressing his chest to her back when the first pulsing beats of Closer by Nine Inch Nails played.

"Hear that, sweetheart?" he growled against her ear. "This song excites our guests like nothing else. Right now, the lights bordering this dropped floor are pulsing to the beat like an invitation... or warning, and whoever wants to will witness you coming on my tongue in about one minute."

"Oh, God."

Gray nipped the juncture of Addie's throat and growled, "What did I tell you about calling for God when I'm the one who makes you come?"

Addie gasped, "You said...there's no God here. Gray...make me come. Please...."

He shifted until he faced the opposite way. Gray's hot breath ghosted over the cleft of her ass when he spread her cheeks apart. He swiped his tongue through her slit until he reached her clit, sucking and flicking her swollen bud over and over.

"Yes...oh, yes...." Addie's core clenched and pulsed on the precipice when her body tensed, and she screamed Gray's name as she tumbled over the edge into the most intense orgasm of her life.

The energy from the crowd she felt watching surged, and Addie fed off the electricity, making her orgasm go on and on.

Gray smacked her ass and then cupped her mound, making her whimper and moan. "Your wet, needy pussy is begging for my cock. Isn't it, sweet girl?"

The mixture of dirty talk and sweet words Gray used drove Addie wild. Her body vibrated, ready to fly apart again. Gray gave her ass another smack when she didn't answer.

Addie shuddered in her restraints. "I'm fucking ready. Please, Gray. I need you to fuck me...need you to claim me."

She wanted Gray to claim her heart and soul.

The rough material of his jeans teased her sensitive flesh when he pressed his groin to the curve of her ass. His hands pressed against her lower back, then he slid them over her shoulders and down her arms, linking their fingers together.

Gray's lips grazed her ear. "The crowd is writhing to the beat. Their focus is on you, anticipating the moment you'll milk my cock of everything I have. Do you sense their hunger, Addie?" Then he growled, "Do you sense mine?"

"Yes...." Addie rocked her hips, relishing the groan of ecstasy she elicited from him.

Gray let go of her right hand, sliding his between them. He unbuttoned and unzipped his jeans, freeing his thick erection. He brushed it against her skin, leaving a trail of precum to her entrance, where he notched the head of his cock.

"Tell me now if you want the blindfold to remain. With your consent, it will come off."

Did she want to see everyone turned on because of her?

Addie knew she wanted Gray to fuck her hard and fill her with his cum. Her pussy tried to suck him deeper. Much to her frustration, Gray refused to give her another inch until she gave him an answer.

He let go of her left hand to cup and fondle her breasts, keeping her on edge while giving her time to contemplate her answer.

Gray tugged and tweaked her nipples, and Addie felt a gush of arousal coat the head of Gray's cock. "Fuck," he growled. "You're dripping down the length of my cock."

Addie wanted Gray. Wanted everyone to know who owned her body and soul. "Take the blindfold off. I want every one of my senses involved."

He nipped her lobe and said the magic words to drive her wild. "Good, girl."

Gray tugged the ribbon, securing the blindfold. It unraveled, falling to the glass floor. He lifted from her back and slammed his cock home while Addie's vision cleared and the writhing, aroused crowd appeared beneath her.

Holy. Fuck.

She pushed back within her restraints, meeting Gray's powerful thrusts. "Yes, take my cock, baby," he encouraged, fucking her harder while a giant orgy unfolded below her.

"Please...make me...I need to come. Please, Gray." Her pleas turned into chants of, "Yes, yes, yes" when he shifted his hips, and his cock rubbed her g-spot on every forward stroke, and Gray circled her clit with his deft fingers. "Ohh...."

"Who do you belong to?"

"You, Gray. Only you. Oh...oh, fuck yes."

"Come for me, Addie."

She exploded and pulsed on his cock, feeling his release spill inside her. Then he pulled free from her pulsing core and unloaded the rest of his cum across her back, marking her as he roared, "I'm yours."

Gray stepped in front of her, stroking his cock, the last of his cum pooling on the tip, which he smeared across her lips. "Open your mouth."

The moment Addie did, Gray pushed past her lips, sliding his cock over her tongue. "Taste how good we are together."

Addie moaned around him, and all too soon, Gray pulled free from her mouth and tucked himself away. He fisted her hair and brought his mouth down on hers, licking her lips to capture the rest of his cum. Then he licked inside her mouth, giving it to her like an offering.

"You're fucking perfect, Addie, and you're mine." He vowed against her parted lips.

"Yours."

The glass floor returned to its previous blacked-out state. Their show finished, and Addie floated in a post-orgasmic haze while Gray undid the cuffs, holding her in place, and wrapped her in the softest blanket, making her mumble and snuggle further into it. He lifted her in his arms and carried her to the couch in the corner.

Gray settled Addie on his lap, tucking the blanket tighter around her before holding a water bottle to her lips. Addie relished the cool liquid trickling down her throat, becoming more aware of her surroundings.

"Are you okay?" His question sent her on a bit of an internal spiral.

Is she okay?

Is getting hit by a freight train — in the best possible way — an appropriate description of okay?

Addie received the best fuck of her life. She's good. More than good.

Is good even a good enough word?

She snorted.

Did she snort?

Happy. Is happy a good enough word? Oops. There's the word good, again.

Her snort became a bout of unstoppable giggles. "I'm fantastic."

"Yeah, you are, sweetheart. Someone's found subspace. You'll be a little loopy, but you're safe. I'm here, and I got you," Gray said, tucking her head beneath his chin and snuggling Addie close. "Chocolate?" he asked, holding out a piece.

"Yes, please."

Gray placed the sweet square on her bottom lip. "Open." She complied, and the rich flavor melted on her tongue.

"Mm. Thank you."

Gray cupped her face and traced his fingertips along her temple, staring into her eyes. Addie stared back, getting lost in the dark depths of his gaze.

Despite the short time she'd known Gray, he'd shown her what being loved was genuinely like.

Love? Fuck yes, she loved him. She's in love with Gray.

Something monumental shifted between them tonight. Gray caressed Addie's parted lips with the whisper of her name, then he kissed her, and her eyelids drifted closed.

CHAPTER TWENTY-FIVE

Addie

A ddie groaned and burrowed deeper beneath the blankets. Her muscles protested, moving even that much. Recovering from body-shattering orgasms is no joke. Her eyelids popped open, and her gaze darted to her cell, where the screen flashed her silenced alarm.

She slept in.

Shit.

Shit. Shit. Shit.

Wrung out after last night, Addie slept the entire drive back to Gray's, rousing when he helped her out of her clothes and into the shower.

That part she remembered vividly.

Gray made her plant her hands on the tile while he washed and conditioned her hair, tending to her reverently like she was his most precious possession.

Addie wanted to be owned, admitting she's head-over-heels for Gray. They needed to talk because something monumental happened last night.

Addie turned her head to find Gray lying face-down, starfish style, on her other side. She'd stolen the blankets, deciding to become a human burrito during the night, and left Gray with a corner of the bedsheet over his hips and thighs.

Oops.

Fuck, he's beautiful.

Addie wanted to stay right there, yet she needed to get up. There are houses to tour, and she'll be late if she doesn't get up. This has been her goal all along.

What if her goals have changed?

Damn it. Addie's supposed to be excited about finding her dream home.

What if she's already living in her dream home, equipped with her dream man, and getting a taste of her dream life?

Addie sighed, then got herself out from the tangle of blankets without waking Gray. She exited the bed with stealth and scrawled a quick note on the pad left on the nightstand.

Off to check out houses. Wish me luck. <smiley face>
A.

Addie tiptoed across the room in nothing except Gray's T-shirt. By now, a good portion of her clothing had migrated from the upstairs closet to Gray's bedroom. Yet, after he'd dried her off last night, Gray dressed her in something of his.

Swoon.

Addie held the collar to her nose, breathing in the fresh laundry smell with a hint of Gray's lingering scent, clenching her thighs when a sudden wave of desire washed over her.

The man smelled like a walking aphrodisiac. Addie wanted to cry because she had no time to enjoy its effect.

Damn it.

Addie needed coffee, then she needed to get her butt in gear to avoid being late to meet the realtor. She slid the bedroom door closed behind her, jumping when she heard:

"Mrrrrrraaaaooooowww."

"Jeez, Minnie." Addie whisper-yelled, clutching at her chest. "Girl, I'm going to get a bell for your collar, then you can't sneak up on me," she scolded, getting over the giant cat's penchant for a good jump-scare. Addie gave Minnie the scratch behind her ear she sought.

"Hungry?"

Minnie's rumbling purr filled the hall. Then the cat sauntered off toward the kitchen, expecting she'd follow.

Cats.

Despite her time restraints, she stayed rooted to the spot. Torn between crawling back into Gray's bed and getting a much-needed cup of coffee to help face the day.

Addie leaned toward the first option, ready to push the bedroom door back open, when her cell buzzed in her hand with a notification from the realtor.

Richard: I know you'll find the perfect house to-day, Addison. The properties I have lined up for you to view are exactly what you're looking for.

Addie dropped her hand from Gray's door. The universe decided for her. She followed Minnie to the kitchen and sent Richard a response.

Addison: Sounds great. I'll meet you at the first address in 45 minutes.

Richard: <thumbs up emoji>

Addie glanced back down the hall at the closed bedroom door with longing while her feet propelled her to the kitchen. This is Gray's house, and she needed to look at these properties.

She needed to do this for herself.

Addie tapped the granite countertop of the third house Richard had shown her, absorbed in her memories of the night before and unable to imagine what it'd be like to own this place or the other two she'd already seen.

Richard said her name, bringing her back to the present. "Sorry, imagining myself baking in this kitchen." Addie figured it was the best way to explain what had to be a dreamy expression on her face.

"Gorgeous, isn't it? Renovated two years ago, the stainless steel appliances are gas...."

Richard's words faded, drowned out by her inner voice chanting, *'None of these places are right. They're not Gray's...they're not home.'*

Addie gasped, gripping the countertop to keep from stumbling. Gray is her home.

"Addison, are you okay?" Richard asked. She remained bent over the counter, taking deep, steadying breaths. "Can I get you some water? Do you need me to call Grayson or someone?"

She straightened, the mention of Gray's name calming her. "What? No. Sorry." Addie shook her head. "Richard, these properties are perfect, but I... I have to go."

"You haven't seen the rest. I promise you will fall in love with the primary suite." Richard stepped back, ready to lead the way, when Addie shook her head again.

"I'm sorry, Richard. I don't need to look at the rest."

"You've made your decision, then? The first house I showed you, right?" A slight desperation entered his tone despite his salesman smile, sensing the loss of an impending deal.

"Not quite."

"What do you mean?" Now, Richard looked straight-up confused. Addie didn't blame him. She was confusing herself at the moment, too.

"I- listen, I know this is last minute, but I need to take care of something, and I can't choose a house until I do."

The urgency to get back to Gray fueled Addie's escape and her words. She grabbed her purse and beat a hasty retreat to the front door with Richard hot on her heels.

"Addison, are you sure there isn't anything-"

Addie glanced at him over her shoulder, not pausing on her way to the door. "Thank you for showing me these properties. I'll contact you with my decision within the next few days."

"Uh-okay. I'll lock up. I'm sure you'll make the right choice for you."

Fuck. Addie hoped she would, too.

"Thank you," she said, closing the car door and waving to the bewildered man through the windshield. Then Addie sped toward Stone Barn Farm.

To Gray.

To home.

CHAPTER TWENTY-SIX

Gray

G ray fucked and claimed Addison Carter in front of the club.

Then Addie said she loved him.

He didn't think she'd remember saying it. He'd heard her, though. Loud and clear. Of course, it came out in the most Addie way possible: a giggle-snort and littered f-bombs.

"Fuck, I fucking love you, Grayson Matthews."

Hell. Addie even full-named him. The passion behind her words fueled the fire within him, and he wanted nothing more than to say it back, yet he hesitated. Addie rode the rush of endorphins last night, and when he kissed her, she crashed, falling asleep in his arms.

She didn't stir when he laid her on the couch. Gray didn't want to leave her, so he stuck his head out the door and called down the hall to Zane, asking him to retrieve their belongings from his office.

Addie roused enough to dress and leave the club, and Gray knew she'd be in no condition to have this conversation. He'd wait until they're both clearheaded.

Except. Gray slept in.

Gray woke and reached for Addie, finding the sheets cold. She must have left a while ago, and he didn't like the reminder of what it'd be like when Addie lived in her own place.

He didn't want to wake up without her ever again.

Gray grabbed his phone, squinting to read the time. Then he rolled across Addie's side of the bed, breathing in her seductive and sweet vanilla scent, and when he sat on the edge of the mattress, Gray saw her note.

Off to check out houses. Wish me luck. <smiley face>
A.

Shit.

Shit. Shit. Shit.

Addie has already left to look at properties with Richard. At this very moment, she could be looking at the house she planned to buy.

Gray looked around his bedroom – the one he now considered his and Addie's – and tried to figure out a way to stop it from happening. He knew deep down Stone Barn Farm belonged to them from the moment Addie walked through his front door. This is their home. He'd call his lawyer and find out what he needed to do to add her to the deed.

He jumped to his feet, ready to get shit done, and winced when his leg protested the sudden movement. Gray massaged the tight muscle and scar tissue, loosening the knots. He needed to grab a hot shower and slather on some cannabis pain ointment, or he'd suffer the consequences later.

The shot of pain brought everything into focus, though. Gray needed to talk to Addie.

He guessed Addie had left an hour ago. There's at least another two hours until she returns.

Please don't let her be an impulse buyer.

Showered, shaved, and dressed in dark denim, a black Henley, a leather shoulder harness, and a matching leather cuff on his left wrist. Gray knew he looked good. He needed every seductive weapon he possessed at his disposal.

Minnie's golden gaze followed Gray while he paced across the living room from her spot on the staircase.

"You like her too. Don't you, Min?" he asked, scratching Minnie's chin. She raised her front paw, offering him a kitty-style high-five.

"Mrrrrrraaaaoooowww."

"I knew you did. Addie's impossible to resist."

Addie is his.

Gray wanted her in his home, his heart, and his bed every single fucking day for the rest of his life. He turned toward the window when he heard a car door slam outside and saw Addie rushing toward the front steps. When she reached the front door, Gray yanked it open and met her on the front steps.

"Don't buy the house." "I love living with you." They said at the same time.

"Wait, what?" "What?" they asked, doing it again, and they both laughed.

Gray pulled Addie into his arms, cupped her face, and kissed her, sweeping his tongue past her lips to tangle with hers, swallowing Addie's sounds.

He broke their kiss and pressed his forehead to hers, speaking the words he'd wanted to say for weeks. "I love you, Addie. Live here with me. Don't buy any of the places you looked at."

"For real? Because I love you, too, and don't want to live anywhere except with you."

Gray tucked a wayward strand of hair behind Addie's ear. He stared into her crystal blue eyes, her gaze filled with love and desire. He knew his eyes reflected the same. "Fuck. Yes." Unable to resist, Gray kissed Addie again.

"Thank fuck. I knew there was a reason I avoided putting an end date on our contract. From the beginning, I never wanted one." Gray's voice filled with possessiveness, and he refused to disguise it.

Addie looped her arms behind Gray's head, running the tips of her fingers through his hair until she settled them at the back of his neck. "Hmm... it'll need amending, though."

Gray caressed her cheek. "It's always open to renegotiation and amendments, sweetheart. What do you have in mind?"

"Locations."

"You mean beyond here and the club?"

She slid her palms down his chest, gripping his leather harness straps tight. "I know Jasper's place is where you stay in the city, which is fine, but it's getting to a point where my career is growing, and I'll need to stay in the city for meetings or events."

"It's a separate apartment, and I know Jasper won't have a problem with you staying there, too."

"And I appreciate the gesture. I want to own the place we stay at in the city." Addie scrunched her brow and looked away, then met his gaze with determination. "Not want, I need to."

Despite her resolve, Gray attempted to convince her otherwise. "Addie, you don't need to-"

She pressed a finger to his lips, stopping the complete insertion of his metaphorical foot into his mouth. "Yes. I do. Listen, I hope we have a lifetime of happiness together...."

Gray dreaded the 'but' Addie left hanging between them, encouraging her to voice it and not shy away. "A lifetime of happiness, but...?"

When she smiled, it captured a tinge of sadness, hurting his heart.

"A lifetime is what I want with you. We've both experienced how it doesn't always work out that way, and I'm not saying we won't, but I need the security of having a place I paid for. You understand, don't you?"

Once again, Gray contemplated finding Addie's ex and fucking him up. He even compiled a mental list of all the excruciating ways he'd do it.

Addie's need for security and independence didn't bother him. "Agreed. Amendment accepted." Gray pulled her tight against him. "Ready to seize the day, love?"

Addie squealed an exuberant "Yes" against his lips when she kissed him. "Are we really doing this?" she asked, peering at him from beneath her lashes.

"Yeah, babe. We're really fucking doing this. You and I are forever, Addie. I'll spend the rest of my life ensuring you never forget it."

CHAPTER TWENTY-SEVEN

Gray

The following Tuesday, Gray rapped on Jasper's open door. "You wanted to talk?"

"I did. How are things going with you, Addison?"

"Never happier. Addie and I...we fit. You know?"

Jasper's stare grew distant, his thumb rubbing the inside of his ring finger. "Yes, I know."

"If anyone does, you do. Hey, um, listen, Addie's agreed to make our temporary living arrangement permanent."

"Congratulations."

"There's one condition."

"Oh? What's the condition?" Jasper asked, meeting Gray's eyes.

"She purchases the place we stay when we're here. It's a security thing for her and something I'm happy to concede to."

Gray shifted, shoving his hands in his pockets. "I won't be needing your basement suite much longer."

Jasper looked away with a sad smile. "It's yours anytime you need it. You and Addison."

"Much appreciated." Gray looked at his friend, and concern filled him. Dark circles dimmed Jasper's hazel eyes, and if he got any sleep, it was in his rumpled clothes.

Jasper hasn't looked this rough since the days following the demise of his marriage.

"I'm pretty sure updating you about my love life isn't why you wanted to talk to me today." Jasper tipped his head toward the door, and Gray took the hint, closing it to give them privacy. "What's going on, Jas?"

Jasper sighed and ran his hand through his messy hair. "I need a favor."

"Of course, brother. It's yours," Gray answered without hesitation.

Jasper chuckled. "You haven't even heard what it is yet."

"Doesn't matter. Whatever you need, it's yours."

"I need to take care of something out of the country, and I need you to take care of the club while I'm gone."

"Done. You going to tell me what this is about?"

Jasper took a fortifying breath, letting out the burden he'd carried for several weeks. "Joanna and Jonathan's surrogate gave birth to their little girl four weeks ago."

"It's a baby girl? Why didn't you tell us?" Gray swallowed, scared to ask his next question after what Jasper's sister and husband went through to conceive. Yet he needed to know. "Is their daughter okay?"

"Yes. For now."

"For now?" Gray's gut twisted.

"The agency Jo and Jon paired with is in the Ukraine."

"Oh. Oh, shit." Gray saw the news coverage this morning and knew how precarious things had become for the country under siege.

"Oh, shit is right, brother. I'm taking the red eye out tonight."

Gray needed to help. Joanna's like a sister to him, which means her little girl is also part of his family. "You can't do this alone. Let me go with you."

Jasper walked around his desk and clasped Gray's shoulders. "Thank you for the offer. What I need to know is everything's taken care of here."

Gray pulled Jasper into a hug. When he released the tight grip on his friend, he asked, "You're sure?"

"Yeah, I've got West on speed dial since he's already in the UK."

Weston Sharpe was the sniper of their crew. His keen eye and lightning-fast reflexes will no doubt keep Jasper and his niece safe. It eased Gray's fear a little.

"Don't do anything stupid, like getting yourself killed."

"Give me a few days, ten at the most, and I'll have my niece in her parent's arms."

"Any longer. I'll lead the cavalry to rescue your ass myself."

Jasper gave him the first genuine smile since Gray walked into his office. "I'd expect nothing less. Take care of our club, and I'll catch you on the flip side."

"You better."

"I will. Promise. I'm gonna head out. Gotta pack and sleep for a couple of hours. Then head to the airport."

"Watch your back."

"Always."

Jasper gathered his wallet and keys from his desk. Gray didn't take his eyes off his friend until he disappeared out the door, and he hoped like hell this wouldn't be a promise Jasper broke.

Epilogue Gray

Six months later.

Gray stayed toward the back of the crowd while Addie finished signing copies of her new release. The stack of books she'd brought dwindled to a couple of copies, soon to sell out, judging by those still waiting to snag one.

An event like this was a first for Club Decadent and those invited. After passing their vetting process, several attendees accepted the invitation to remain guests for the night when the club opened.

The joy radiating from Addie surrounded Gray when their eyes met. "I love you," he mouthed. He saw her cheeks warm from across the room when she smiled and mouthed "I love you" back.

When he met Addison Carter, their lives melded with ease; loving her is as natural for Gray as breathing, and he never wanted to let her go. And tonight, he planned an epic claiming right after he did one other crucial thing....

When Addie introduced Gray to her daughter, Sadie, thankfully, they hit it off.

Gray came into the city alone two weeks ago while Addie stayed at the farm. Not something they often did since making their living arrangement permanent, but she wanted to work on her next manuscript, and when Addie's in the zone with the words flowing, there's no stopping her.

It allowed Gray to get together with Sadie to tell her he wanted to marry Addison.

Gray didn't ask for permission or Sadie's blessing. Addie's the only person able to give him those. He did, however, vow to cherish her mother and honor her the way she deserved for the rest of their lives.

Over dinner, Sadie told him a bit about her childhood. How Addie did her best to protect her from the bad things, showing her all the love a kid ever wanted. She still witnessed the way her father mistreated her mother.

Fuck, he wanted to destroy Addie's ex.

Then Sadie said something to make Gray emotional. She told him she'd never seen her mother more happy or in love.

Sadie got up from her chair, and Gray did, too. They hugged it out in the middle of the busy restaurant, and when they sat back down, Sadie smiled, and with a spark reminding him of Addie, she gave him her blessing, anyway.

Gray may never want children of his own, but he's gonna rock the shit out of being a stepdad.

If Addie says yes.

Fuck, the nerves are getting to him. The good kind, mixed with excitement and love for what's coming. *Seize the day?* No. Gray planned to seize the rest of his life with Addie.

With the last book signed, Addie thanked everyone for coming before seeking Gray out. A grin lit up his face, and he unleashed the full effect of his dimples, knowing what they did to his girl.

The way Addie bit her bottom lip while he approached told him he'd find her panties soaked if they weren't in his desk drawer. Gray imagined Addie's arousal coating her folds and bare thighs like a naughty little secret.

Gray made it to the stage and stopped Addie from descending the stairs. He pulled her close and devoured her mouth in a heated kiss. "Mm... hello, beautiful," he greeted when they came up for air.

"Hello to you too," came Addie's breathless response.

"Missed you," he said, leaning in for another kiss.

Addie stopped him with a playful smack to his chest and whispered, "How did you have time? You had me bent over your desk a couple of hours ago."

Gray bent her over his desk all right. Addie came on his tongue while he ate her from behind like a dying man who found his oasis in the desert. Gray then sent Addie out to the waiting crowd with lusty satisfaction all over her face.

"You seemed nervous, and I wanted to relieve your stress. And in case you aren't aware, I'll never get enough of you, Ms. Carter."

Addie's eyes shimmered, and she blinked back her tears. "I love you, Gray."

"I'm fucking so glad you do," he said with a laugh.

It's time.

Gray took a deep breath and slowly let it out. He slipped his hand into the inside pocket of his jacket, grabbing one of the two items he'd tucked next to his heart. Then he used the table to help lower himself onto his good knee while Addie stared at him, aghast.

"What are you doing?" she whisper-yelled, glancing at their smiling audience.

"What does it look like I'm doing?" Gray whisper-yelled back, holding out the little blue box. "I'm asking you to marry me."

"Here? Now?" Addie asked, eyeing the blue box he'd yet to pop open.

Throughout their time together, Addie became more confident and self-assured in her storytelling abilities. She told him about her process and discussed her work with more confidence.

Gray also paid attention to the details.

A Tiffany princess-cut diamond gets mentioned anytime Addie's characters get engaged. When Gray lifted the lid of the little blue box, he let the perfect two-carat diamond sparkle under the stage lights.

"Yes, I'm asking here and now. What better place to seize the rest of our days than the one where you ran into me and changed my life forever? I love you, Addie. Marry me and share the rest of your life with me."

Addie's eyes glistened with tears. "I'd love nothing more than to be your wife and partner. Yes, I'll marry you. I love you, Gray." He slipped the band onto her ring finger, and with a bit of help from her and the table, Gray rose to his feet.

Gray held her. "I love you so fucking much," he said, staring into her eyes and catching a wayward tear on her cheek with his thumb. "Hey, the only tears you're shedding tonight are the ones you gift me when you choke on my dick in front of all these people."

Addie whimpered against his lips, and Gray pressed his forehead to hers. He dropped his voice to the deep baritone he knew would send shivers down her spine. "Such a good girl. Will you accept my collar and let me claim you in front of everyone?"

"Yes. Please, Gray. I want your ring and your collar." Addie declared loud and clear. "Claim me."

Gray tucked the jewelry box back in his pocket and pulled out the leather collar he'd made for Addie. He tossed his jacket aside, revealing his fitted button-down and favorite leather harness. Gray unbuttoned his shirt cuffs and rolled the sleeves to his elbows.

Addie bit her bottom lip while her gaze tracked his movements.

He designed the collar with a locking mechanism on the back and a small O-ring at the front. When he flipped it over in his palm, Addie traced their names, which he carved along the inside.

"Will you accept my collar and be mine? Let me give you all the love and pleasure you can take."

"It's beautiful, and I'm honored to accept. Within the parameters of our agreement," Addie said with a hint of sass.

A possessive rumble came from deep within Gray's chest when Addie lifted her braid and turned to let him fasten it around her throat.

Gray ran his finger beneath the edge, checking the fit. "Perfect." He clasped her shoulders and kissed the base of her throat where her new collar caressed her skin. "How do you feel?"

"Mm...powerful and sexy." Addie spun around to face him. "I'm powerful and sexy."

Gray held her face between his palms and kissed her. "You are Addie and so much more. I'm not sure which turns me on the most. My ring on your finger or my collar around your neck."

"Can't it be both?"

"Oh, it's definitely both."

Addie's gaze dipped to the bulge straining beneath his zipper, then she met his gaze from beneath her lashes and asked, "Is it my turn to claim you?"

"Fuck, yes. Go to the center of the stage and get on your knees." Gray waited until Addie settled on her heels and met his gaze. Then he walked toward her, grasping Addie's chin, and asked, "Ready, babe?"

"Yes. Please, Gray. I need to taste you."

"Then take my cock out."

"Yes, sir." Addie unzipped his pants and took his erection into her hand.

"You don't need to hold it, baby. Keep your hands on my thighs."

Addie licked her lips. "Yes, sir."

"What will you do if your mouth's occupied and you need me to stop?"

"I'll tap your thigh twice or pinch you if I need you to stop. Red if I can speak. For the record, I'm green, sir."

Gray tilted her head back with his hand in her hair and growled, "My sassy good girl. Open your mouth and show me your tongue."

Oblivious to the growing excitement of the crowd, Gray rested the head of his cock on her outstretched tongue, rubbing his precum against her tastebuds, making Addie moan.

"Suck the tip," he commanded. Then it was Gray's turn to moan when Addie's swollen lips wrapped around his crown, sucking him hard and flicking her tongue against his slit.

Gray tightened his grip on her hair, and Addie relaxed her jaw, taking him deeper until he kissed the back of her throat.

Addie gagged, then swallowed around him, giving Gray those sweet mascara tears he craved.

"My gorgeous, perfect girl."

His balls drew tight, and Gray fucked Addie's face harder, slipping into her throat a little further each time. Addie never took her eyes off him, smiling around his dick at one point, encouraging him to go deeper.

"Take everything I have, baby. You're such a good girl, Addie. My good girl," he said as the first spurts of his release pulsed down Addie's throat.

Gray pulled back and jacked the rest onto her waiting tongue, painting her lips with the last drops. "No one will ever doubt who owns me, heart and soul. I love you, Addie."

Addie licked her lips and swallowed the rest of his release. "I love you, too." Gray tucked himself away. Then he pulled Addie into his arms, kissing her, chasing the taste of himself on her tongue.

Reality came knocking when others reaching their pinnacle penetrated their desire-filled haze. Gray gave Addie a rueful smile when he clasped her hand and kissed her knuckles.

Now that the public part of the evening was over, Gray wanted Addie to himself. "Come on, sweetheart. Let me give you some aftercare."

Kari wiped a tear from the corner of her eye. "I better get the story now, Gray." She leaned against the railing outside Jasper's office and relished Addie's accepting Gray's proposal.

There's no mistaking the shift in the energy in the club. Kari felt the club's energy change, and her gaze returned to the stage. She gasped when Addie accepted Gray's collar and then got down on her knees for him.

The distance obscured the finer details. Kari got the gist, though.

She released a sigh filled with longing. Kari loved to be the center of attention and yearned to be adored. Yet she worked here for over a year and never took part, keeping her desires under wraps. It's how Kari got through the last two years. Now she wanted to try. Maybe approach a Dom on her night off....

Kari leaned further over the rail, getting lost in the couple center stage. When a throat cleared behind her, she almost lost her balance.

Until a set of powerful hands wrapped around Kari's arms, saving her from certain death to lean against a solid wall of muscle. The tiny version of a sexy schoolgirl uniform she wore offered little material to separate them.

"You looking for trouble, little girl?" Her rescuer growled into her ear. The deep gravel of his voice, with the hint of an accent, made her shiver.

Kari turned her head, letting her gaze travel over the sexiest man she'd ever encountered. A man she almost equaled in height, thanks to her stacked Mary Jane's. While she fought the desperate urge to whimper, '*With you? Yes, Daddy.*' Kari let her inner brat take over and said, "Who are you calling little?"

Thank You

Thank you for reading. If you enjoyed this book, please consider leaving a review on Amazon and/or Goodreads. Reviews help Indie Authors so much, and I appreciate every one of you. Happy Reading!

Also by K.C. Ford

Club Decadent Series

One Night at Club Decadent (prequel) (MF/FF/FFM/MFM/MMF Married Couple Polysexual Romance)

Their Protective Dom Bk 1(MMF Bodyguard Sword-Crossing Age-Gap Romance)

Addie & Gray Bk 2 (MF Older Woman/Younger Man Romance)

Jess & Jasper Bk 3 (MF Second-Chance Married Couple Romance)

Their Valentine Dom (novella) (MMF Holiday Smut-filled Romance)

Kari & West Bk 4 Coming Soon (MF Bi4Bi Age-Gap Romance)

Their Primal Dom (novella) (MMF Primal Play Lactation Kink Smut-Filled Romance) Coming Soon

One Weekend in Connecticut (novella) (MF/MMMF/MFM/MMF Married Couple Polysexual Romance) Coming Soon

Standalones – Wide Releases Available Everywhere

The Contract (novella) (MMF Married Couple Cuckhold Bi-Awakening Romance)

It Started with a Gym Crush (MF Older Woman/Younger Man Age-Gap Romance) Coming Soon

Follow Me

Follow my Amazon Author Page to get notified of my latest release.

<u>K.C. Ford Author Page</u>

Visit my website for First Chapter Previews, Content Warnings, and Bonus Chapters.

Author K.C. Ford Website

www.ingramcontent.com/pod-product-compliance
Lightning Source LLC
Chambersburg PA
CBHW050354260626
47156CB00003B/728